Turning the Tables

an Italian Connection novel

Joan Kilby

Entangled Publishing, LLC
2614 South Timberline Road
Suite 109
Fort Collins, CO 80525
Visit our website at www.entangledpublishing.com.

Brazen is an imprint of Entangled Publishing, LLC. For more information on our titles, visit www.brazenbooks.com.

Edited by Vanessa Mitchell
Cover design by Heather Howland
Cover art by iStock

Manufactured in the United States of America

First Edition June 2015

Chapter One

Tina Borlenghi, cushioned in the limo's luxurious interior, rested a hand on the box of pastries by her side and peered out the tinted window for a first glimpse of her flagship American store, a Madison Avenue fashion boutique.

All the bad stuff with Fabio and the court case was behind her. Through her dark days of heartbreak and humiliation, she'd focused on her work as a way of coping. Now it was paying off. New York. New start. Life was becoming good again.

And why shouldn't it? She was launching her atelier, the House of Borlenghi, personally overseeing the opening of the new boutique *and* showing her new collection during fashion week.

The limo negotiated the morning rush hour traffic and glided to a halt at the curb. Marble columns flanked double glass doors on a store occupying a highly desirable corner location. The name, Borlenghi Boutique, was hand-painted in flowing ivory script. Her smile spread. "*Bella*."

The uniformed driver got out and opened her door, offering her a gloved hand to help her onto the sidewalk of the busy street. "Ma'am."

"*Grazie*...." She glanced at his kindly, avuncular face. "What is your name?"

"Frank, ma'am." He handed her the card bearing his phone number. "Contact me when you're ready to move on."

"Okay, and please, call me Tina." She gave him a smile and turned to the boutique.

The doors were locked and the CLOSED sign turned out. Tina knocked on the glass, then smoothed down her taupe linen sheath with russet accents that picked up the highlights in her brown hair. This dress, one she'd designed herself, was a flattering cut. Ever since all the drama with Fabio she couldn't stop eating pastries and had put on a few pounds.

The sudden piercing whine of a power saw drew her attention to the sports bar next door on the side street. HAT TRICK, the sign read. The rustic wooden door was propped open and a well-tracked canvas cloth was laid down at the entrance.

The boutique door opened, reclaiming her attention. A blond woman with perfectly styled hair ushered her inside. "Bettina Borlenghi?" She pressed a splayed hand to her chest where a string of freshwater pearls gleamed against a chic black dress. "I'm Charmaine Denton. Welcome to Manhattan. It's such a delight to meet you! A great, great honor and a thrill."

"Call me Tina." Tina embraced her New York agent, kissing her on both cheeks. She almost felt she knew Charmaine because they'd emailed back and forth for months, but this was their first face-to-face meeting. "It's lovely to meet you."

She glanced around the elegantly outfitted boutique, a plush realm of cream carpets, silk wallpaper and soft music. A water feature tinkled quietly, surrounded by live ferns and marble statuary. "Oh, my, it's beautiful."

Tina presented Charmaine with the white box from one of the best bakeries in New York. "Pastries for you and the staff. It's a custom in Italy."

"Thank you so much. I'm sure they're delicious." Charmaine passed a slender hand over her tiny waist and then placed the box on the glass display counter. She glanced wistfully at it. "I'll have one later."

"Where is everyone—the manager, the sales assistants?" Tina asked.

"The sales girls won't be in until tomorrow when we have the grand opening," Charmaine said. "They've completed all the requisite training, and I put them through their paces earlier today. Janelle, your manager, would have been here today, but her elderly mother had a fall. Janelle had to take her for X-rays."

"I'm sorry to hear that. Can you arrange flowers? I'll call her later." Tina strolled through the store. Clothing racks and display cases were stocked with her latest designs, the autumn collection she'd had sent over from Rome. Now and then she paused to position the hanging garments more evenly. "The showroom looks wonderful. Janelle and her assistants have done a fine job."

"Did you have a chance to go over the itinerary I sent you?" Charmaine got out her phone and started scrolling. "Tomorrow you have a radio interview at seven am, followed by a press conference at nine. Lunch with the editor of Vogue and then we'll sit down with the event manager and go over last minute details of the fashion show. The casting agent has the models lined up as well as our official photographer. The press will be there, of course."

"Who is…the photographer?" *Please don't let it be Fabio.* Tina's hand tightened around the cold stainless steel tube of a display rack. This being fashion week in New York, it was quite likely he was in town. He'd escaped a jail sentence in Italy, but surely he wouldn't seek a job with her company again. She should have told Charmaine under no circumstances to hire him, but that would have meant humiliating explanations.

"Jason Whitely," Charmaine said. "He's excellent."

"*Va bene.*" Fine. Tina released her held breath and resumed her tour. The three fitting rooms were as spacious and luxurious as the rest of the store. Ridiculous that even the thought of Fabio could still upset her so. The past was the past. She would never be so stupid as to fall for a fortune-hunter again.

She paused in front of the three big display windows fronting onto Madison Avenue. As per her instructions, they were empty, awaiting her personal attention. Diaphanous fabric in autumn hues covered the tiered platforms that would hold three mannequins in each window. Nine in all. Daywear, cocktail/evening wear, maybe a weekend in the country….

"I called a handyman to move the mannequins into the windows," Charmaine said. "Or rather, I left a message with the temp agency. He should be here soon." She paused. "Dressing all these mannequins will be a lot of work. I know you said you wanted to do it yourself but are you sure you don't want me to call in a couple of the girls to help?"

"No, thank you. I've been looking forward to this. One of my first jobs in the industry was as a window dresser." She missed the creativity of putting together a beautiful tableau. It was almost like therapy after the business side of her life. And this store symbolized her personal rise from the ashes, a new beginning. It felt important that she have a hand in contributing to the opening.

"Well, okay." Charmaine fingered her pearls, adjusting the diamanté clasp. "But keep the closed sign on the door. With no salesgirls on duty you don't want to be bothered with customers."

Tina adjusted the drape of the cloth on one of the platforms. "Oh, but it would be fun to make the very first sale of my new boutique myself."

"Can you work a cash register?" Charmaine asked doubtfully.

"Poof!" Tina flapped a hand. "I helped in my father's furniture store from the age of twelve." Her dad had been a self-made man, and although he'd skyrocketed to success building a business empire, he'd always made sure his children were grounded growing up. Pocket money had to be earned. Tina and her brother and two sisters had all worked from an early age. "Where are the rest of the clothes, the ones I earmarked for the windows?"

"The store room is this way." Charmaine wove through the display racks to the rear of the boutique and opened a door in the trompe l'oeil mural of the Uffizi Gardens. More racks of clothes waited along with a collection of mannequins. "Janelle had the girls touch the garments up with a steamer. Accessories are in those boxes."

"Excellent." Tina eyed the tall, heavy mannequins. "When did you say the handyman was coming?"

"He should be here any minute." Charmaine checked her watch. "I'm sorry, but I can't stay to deal with him for you. I have to go. I'm already late for a meeting with the event manager at Lincoln Center to discuss the fashion show."

"No problem. I can let him know what I'd like him to do." She led the way back through the store, already feeling a proprietary pride, and out the wide glass doors to the sidewalk. Now the sound of hammering came from next door. "What's going on there?"

"Must be some renovations. I hope they're done by tomorrow for your opening." Charmaine stepped to the curb and hailed a passing yellow taxi. "Let me quickly finish telling you about the rest of the marketing campaign. Flyers will be delivered in all five boroughs tomorrow. The day after, half the buses in New York will be driving around with an ad for the House of Borlenghi on their sides. You know, the one you posed for."

"I remember." She'd felt extremely silly at the time — she was no model — but she supposed Charmaine knew what she was doing.

"I, or Janelle, will be around later to lock up." A taxi pulled up and stopped. Charmaine opened the door. "If you need anything just call me."

"I will be fine." Tina sent her off with another set of kisses. "*Mille grazie. Ciao ciao.*"

She glanced up and down Madison, hoping to see the handyman arriving. Aside from an electrician's van parked around the corner next to the sports bar, there was no tradesman's vehicle anywhere on the horizon. Very well, she would try to move the mannequins herself.

Back inside she exchanged her high heels for a pair of ballet flats from the shoe display and her good dress for the plainest skirt and top she could find. Then she wound her long, waving dark hair into a messy knot and pinned it to the top of her head. Wrapping both her arms around a mannequin she tried to lift it. The six-foot plastic statue wouldn't budge. *Allora*, she would drag it. Rising onto her tiptoes she hooked her arms through the elbows set akimbo and tried to back up, hauling backward with all her might.

The mannequin started to topple, and she staggered under the weight. *Madre mia*, but it was heavy. The bell over the door chimed. She glanced over her shoulder to see a workman in dusty jeans and scuffed boots enter the store. Tall with broad shoulders, he looked strong.

"Thank God." She shifted the weight on her aching shoulders. "I'm so glad to see you."

He lifted the mannequin off her and casually stood it upright. Tina cast him a sidelong glance. Not just any workman, this guy was handsome. Dark blond messy hair, rugged good looks, his white T-shirt stretched tight across a well-developed chest and sculpted biceps. A tool belt was slung from narrow hips, dragging faded snug jeans just low enough to reveal a narrow band of black underwear.

Puzzled blue eyes studied her. "You were expecting me?"

"Charmaine called you." Tina dusted off her hands and her skirt. "She left a message."

"I didn't get it." He shrugged. "Is Charmaine your boss?

I'd like to talk to her, or whoever's in charge."

"I'm in charge," Tina said. "I need you to move these mannequins into the display windows."

He scratched his head. "Well, now, I don't know…"

"You don't know?" She wasn't used to anyone questioning her orders. A long trailing curl escaped from her topknot and tickled her jaw. She brushed it back impatiently. "Aren't you the handyman?"

An "aha" expression dawned. His eyes twinkled as he slowly and blatantly checked her out. Then his deep drawl, laden with humor, poured over her like warm molasses. "Honey, I'll be anyone you want me to be."

Whoa. What was going on here?

Tina bit her lip, noting his small smile with a hint of dimple in his right cheek. Was he *flirting* with her? The thought gave her an unexpected thrill. She pushed that aside. She was busy and had no time for such nonsense. Anyway, probably she was mistaken. Her English was fluent, but she didn't always understand nuances. If he *was* flirting, though, his openness was refreshing. Most men waited for her to make the first move.

Anyone you want me to be… Without even knowing her, he'd somehow tapped into her secret desire to role play even though she'd never met anyone she trusted enough to do it with. But no, he couldn't mean it, not that way. He seemed harmless—except for that lethal twinkle in his eyes. Why not play along? Tapping a finger against her chin, she said thoughtfully, "I would like you to be…a Highland warrior."

"Oh, darn." He clicked his fingers. "I left my broadsword at home. And my kilts are at the cleaners."

Tina gave a sigh of mock exasperation. "Then you'll

have to be a handyman."

"Then that's who I am." With a shrug and a smile, he held out his hand. "Luke."

"Tina B—" She caught herself. Her last name was a household word in Italy, and she hated the fuss it caused. In America, outside an elite fashion circle, very few had heard of her. She liked that but knew it wouldn't last. Her name was on the storefront and soon the marketing program would be in full swing. For now, though, she enjoyed being anonymous. "Just Tina."

His hand engulfed hers, callused, warm and strong. Her gaze drifted down his strong body to his scuffed steel-toe work boots. So different from Fabio. Here was a man who earned his keep from the labor of his own hands instead of sponging off wealthy women. She glanced up again, and his gaze caught hers, lingering too long.

"So," Luke said finally, clearing his throat. "The mannequins."

"*Sì, sì.*" She tugged her hand away and briskly stepped aside.

Luke picked up the mannequin and tucked it under his arm. A ghost of a suggestive smile lifted his lips. "Where do you want it?"

Anywhere you want to give it to me. Goodness, where had that come from? She didn't even know the man! Although she wouldn't mind getting to know him better…

The absurdity of her thoughts washed over her. But after wasting so much time and emotional energy on Fabio, she welcomed finally feeling a spark with someone new. Was that so wrong? Whether she started something or not, this delicious little sizzle of attraction proved that she was alive.

That she'd survived.

He raised a brow in her direction. *Sì*. Right. The mannequin. "Over there, in the first window," she directed. He carried it out there. "On top of the platform. Yes, like so. *Perfetto*!"

Luke went back for another, hoisting it as easily as if it was a log for the fire. "You shouldn't have tried to carry these yourself. There are safety laws against shop assistants doing heavy lifting." He winked over his shoulder at her. "I wouldn't want you to hurt yourself."

"I'm not—" She started to correct him and then stopped. He thought she was a shop assistant. Not surprising, really, considering she'd changed her clothes and her hair. Of course she was doing what an employee would normally do. She should correct Luke's misconception…but telling him she was the boss would no doubt wipe that cheeky smile off his handsome face. She really liked that cheeky smile and what it meant. Open, friendly, and frankly admiring, his smile said he liked her even though he didn't know who she was. Until Fabio she'd never questioned whether she was attractive in her own right and not just because of her money or heritage. Finding out that her ex hadn't loved her but had only been using her had unearthed an insecurity she hadn't even known she possessed. It had gotten so she didn't trust anyone except her family and old friends. Now she questioned every relationship, every new friendship. The fears ran so deep, they opened a terrifying chasm of self-doubt whenever she met someone new.

Where was the harm in letting Luke think she was a sales girl? Once he finished this task she would likely never see him again. If she kept quiet, for the next half hour or so she could enjoy a harmless flirtation with a hot guy. A guy who didn't bow and scrape and make her wonder if he really liked her or if he was only pretending because of who she was. Or how much she was paying him. *Dio*, she sounded so pathetic when she thought like that.

"I'm glad you're here to help," she said. "I have to get all these mannequins into the window and dressed before tomorrow."

"No worries." Luke started to set the second mannequin in place.

"Wait. I need to make sure they're evenly spaced." Tina hesitated, then boldly grabbed him by his tool belt and with her other hand plucked the square metal tape measure from its leather holder.

"Your boss a perfectionist, is she?" Luke didn't seem to mind her taking liberties, just watched her with a bemused expression that turned her cheeks rosy. "A bit of a pain in the butt, sounds like."

"I am n—" Tina began indignantly, then quickly amended, "I mean *she's* not a pain. She cares passionately about her designs and wants them shown off to their best advantage. I would do the same—if I were in her position, that is."

"You're defending her which proves you're nice. But I, for one, am glad you're not the boss." He gave her his dimpled smile again. "Rich women don't give handymen the time of day."

Tina had to bite her tongue not to respond. That was so unfair. She was polite and friendly to everyone she met. But he couldn't be talking about her. He didn't even know her.

She marked out the spacing and adjusted the pedestals to within a quarter of an inch. "Everything must be just so.

If not, the eye will detect a flaw without knowing what is wrong."

"True, the same kind of thing applies in building construction." When she was satisfied, Luke positioned the mannequin. He glanced from the height of it on the platform to her five foot six inches. "I'll get a step ladder from the store room."

"I'll bring out the rack of clothes." She put an extra sway in her hips as she led the way toward the store room, conscious of him following closely behind. "After you finish getting the mannequins, I'll need these boxes, too."

"Your wish is my command." Luke bowed low. But as he straightened, there was that wink again, silently mocking his pretend deference.

Tina blinked. Did handymen in America always behave this way? Maybe she should be offended, but instead she admired his confidence. When he passed her carrying the step ladder his arm lightly brushed against hers. She didn't think it was accidental, and he didn't apologize. The touch of heat drew her gaze to his. The look that passed between them made her breath catch.

This was crazy. And so not what she'd imagined happening on her first day in New York. Maybe she was jet-lagged. Or needy after Fabio's betrayal. Whatever the reason, she needed to make sure the flirtation didn't get out of hand. After all, she was the boss. While he was intriguing, she didn't want him to think he could take advantage of her good nature. That was never going to happen again.

Work, she needed to get to work.

She left him to his various tasks and went to the washroom to scrub her hands clean before handling the garments.

When she returned, the stepladder was in place, the boxes moved, and he'd resumed transporting the remaining mannequins.

Tina chose a dress from the rack and carried it up the ladder. She dropped it carefully over the mannequin's head, draping the life-like figurine with fine Italian wool in shades of black and forest green. With straight pins placed invisibly, she adjusted the fit.

"Nice duds." Luke handed her a dropped pin. "I don't know much about women's fashions but I can tell these are classy."

"*Grazie!*" she said, beaming. At the House of Borlenghi, she employed a team of designers but this was another dress she'd sketched the pattern of herself. "It's one of my own—" Designs. To cover her near gaff she made an extravagant gesture that wobbled the ladder. "One of my *favorites.*"

"Careful." Luke put a steadying hand on her leg, lingering just a touch too long—and yet, somehow not long enough—before he removed it. "Your boss should pay you double for that kind of enthusiasm."

Maybe she was being a little over the top for someone not invested in the brand. More subdued, she climbed down and rummaged through a large, many-tiered box of high quality costume jewelry she'd had sent over from Rome, selecting an amber-colored pendant on a long gold chain. Climbing back up, she draped it on the mannequin.

Out of the corner of her eye, she could see Luke making minor adjustments until he was satisfied the mannequins looked right. Clearly he was also a perfectionist. She admired the easy way he moved, like a man accustomed to doing physical work. Or like an athlete. His muscular forearms were covered in a thin layer of dark golden hair. His hands were large and strong. His thighs were like tree trunks. That butt could be carved in marble and made into a Roman statue fit for the Vatican museum.

He caught her staring as he stepped out of the window, and his eyes crinkled knowingly. "Anything else you'd like me to do while I'm here?"

What a loaded question. What if she said she'd like to take him into the fitting room and strip him down to his tool belt? Straddle him naked on the lilac velvet settee surrounded by a three-way mirror?

"No, that's all." Her voice was cool but her body, suddenly, was hot. "*Grazie*, you did a good job."

He hesitated. "It's going to take you forever going up and down that ladder. Tell me what you want from that box, I can hand it up to you."

"That isn't a handyman's job." Was he as reluctant to leave as she was to see him go?

"Hey, anyone who can lease a boutique in this neighborhood must have mega-bucks. You shouldn't worry about this Charmaine dame paying for another hour or two of my time."

Her temperature cooled instantly. Oh, so he wanted to draw out the hours he got paid, did he? "Just because someone is well off doesn't mean they should be cheated."

Luke's eyes widened, then narrowed. "Just because someone has money doesn't mean they own people. Maybe you're prepared to be treated like a slave, but I'm not."

"So you *are* trying to pad the bill." Furious and disappointed, she turned away.

"Hell, no. I just wanted to help. You're all alone here

with some hard-assed boss overworking you." He raised a hand and took a step backward. "Never mind, I'll get going."

Oh, dear. How had their buzzing flirtation flipped so quickly into antagonism? He'd pushed her buttons. But maybe she was wrong. It wasn't fair to judge a stranger just because Fabio had swindled her. She had to stop being so suspicious.

"Wait, I'm sorry." She reached out and touched his arm. "I jumped to conclusions."

He stiffened at first and then blew out a gusty sigh. "It's okay. Let's back up."

"Please, have a pastry before you go." She opened the box and pushed it toward him. Maybe it was because she was Italian but when she liked someone, she wanted to feed them. Plus she was liable to eat all the pastries herself if he didn't help. "*Mangia*."

"Well…I never say no to pastry." He reached for a sugared confection oozing blueberries and custard. Tina selected an almond Danish. The atmosphere returned to calm. "*Mangia*. That's Italian, right?"

"*Sì*. I'm from Rome." Her gaze followed as he carried the pastry to his mouth and sank his teeth into the flaky crust.

Luke chewed and swallowed. "I thought I detected an accent. Your English is very good. How long have you been living in the US?"

"N-not long." If she told him she was only here temporarily it would lead to more questions, questions she didn't want to answer. "I studied English in school." And she traveled the world for her work often resorting to English as a universal language. She wiped the crumbs from her lip with a fingertip, followed by her tongue.

Luke's gaze riveted on her mouth. "You have a bit of sugar, right…here." He brushed the corner of her bottom lip with his thumb, making her skin tingle.

"*Grazie*," she said, huskily, suddenly shy.

"You have a sexy voice. I love the way you roll your R's."

"*I tuoi occhi sono molto azzurro.*" Your eyes are very blue. Deliberately, she drew out the long rolling R.

"Oh, man, you're killing me." He shut his eyes, half smiling, half groaning, and leaned toward her to brush his mouth across hers lightly.

She shouldn't respond…but she couldn't stop herself. Didn't want to. Tina tilted her head up and tasted. He was sweet and salty, a deliciously addictive combination. She drew back, murmuring, "I never knew American handymen had so many talents."

"About that…" He nuzzled her neck. "I have a confession to make."

Her eyes snapped open. Oh no. Not a confession. Confessions meant wrong-doing. She stepped back. Couldn't she have a simple interaction with a sexy guy who liked her for no other reason than that he liked her? She put down her pastry. "Tell me."

"Whoa, don't look so fierce. It's nothing earth-shattering. Just, I'm not a handyman."

"You lied to me?" Her nostrils flared on an inhale. Fabio had lied to her too. He'd also cheated on her and conned her out of a good chunk of cash. She and her family had been publicly humiliated by the tabloid press when the affair was dragged through the courts. Worst of all, he'd made her feel bad about herself, stupid and fat and foolish. "Who are you?"

"I'm from next door at the sports bar." He hooked a thumb over his shoulder. "I just came over to apologize for all the noise."

Mechanically, she closed the pastry box and retied the string. She couldn't even begin to imagine what Luke had hoped he would get from her. The fact that he'd lied was deeply disappointing. "Thank you for your consideration."

He leaned in, trying to catch her eye. "Hey, I'm sorry. I didn't think it was a big deal. You were the one who started it with your fantasy man."

No, he'd started it by telling her he'd be anything she wanted him to be. Maybe she should have requested he be an honorable man, or was that too big a dream? "Your boss will be wondering where you are," she said pointedly.

He grinned, all cocky and charming. "Yeah, well, he's a pretty good guy. It'll be okay."

She struggled to hold onto her indignation, but it wasn't easy. After all she'd concealed her identity as well, and *still* wasn't telling him the truth for fear of destroying the delicious sexual tension shimmering between them. Reluctantly, she asked, "What's funny?"

"I'm the boss. I own the bar."

"But you're dressed as a workman. I don't understand."

"The contractor doing the reno on the kitchen was short a guy today." Luke shrugged. "Years ago I used to work in construction so I picked up a hammer."

"Why didn't you simply tell me that?"

"And miss an opportunity to help a pretty lady?" The teasing light in his eyes was back. He tucked a strand of curling dark hair behind her ear and let his fingertips trail down her neck, making her skin tingle in their wake.

"You're just flattering me." God help her, she loved it. She preened like a cat being stroked. Any second now she'd be purring.

"It's not flattery if it's true."

He sounded sincere. She didn't know what to say. This man wasn't Fabio. He didn't even know she had any money so how could he be after it? Their argument about billing hours was completely moot since he'd volunteered his time. She'd overreacted—understandable given her history, but it wasn't fair to Luke.

"And…" His voice dropped to a low rumble. "I liked the way you ordered me around."

Oh. The veiled sexual implications did funny things to her stomach. Made her think of a thousand possibilities. A slow smile curled her lips. "I've had a lot of experience at that."

"Interesting." He placed his hands on either side of her, trapping her with her back to the counter. His eyes were only inches away, bright blue with flecks of navy. Mesmerizing. "Let me make it up to you. Have dinner with me. After we eat you could tell me what to do some more."

"I…I can't." Was she holding her breath? Was that why she couldn't breathe? If she leaned forward half an inch the bodice of her dress would brush his T-shirt.

"Why?"

A million reasons. She was busy with the launch. She was still hurting and humiliated. She had no intention of starting something with a man when she was only here for a brief period, no matter how much he stirred her blood or made her feel alive. But with Luke's breath fanning her forehead and the heat from his body warming her even though they weren't touching, reason wasn't the strongest force operating inside her right now.

Just a fling, a little voice whispered in her head. *You're only here for a week. You're virtually anonymous. No one will know, or care when it's over.* Luke would be fun, uncomplicated. An antidote to her self-doubt after Fabio.

She had just enough presence of mind to remember her early morning radio interview. "It's not a good idea. I can't stay out late. I have to be at work early."

"That slave-driving boss again. I will definitely have to talk with her." Luke bumped his nose against hers. "I could pick you up at seven, have you home by ten."

"You are very determined, aren't you?"

"It's my defining trait. Where do you live?"

She was staying at the St. Regis Hotel, but she could hardly tell him that, not after letting him think she was a sales assistant and a resident of New York. "Thank you, but no."

"You're breaking my heart." He flashed her a smile so dazzling she had to bite her tongue not to instantly retract her refusal. Then he fished a business card out of his shirt pocket and placed it in her palm, wrapping her fingers around it. "If you change your mind, call me."

"Okay. I mean, no." Slightly dazed, she watched him walk to the door. "*Ciao*."

Madre mia. He was hot, he was nice, and he didn't want a single thing from her. Well, except for the obvious. Frankly, she could do with a little of that, herself.

But she'd done the right thing in saying no. Hadn't she?

Chapter Two

Luke got five paces away from the boutique, and his feet wouldn't carry him any farther. He couldn't leave it like that. Tina was more interesting than any woman he'd met in a very long time. Maybe ever. Okay "ever" was a big call but still…

He turned around and walked back inside to find her hanging clothes on a rack, handling the garments with as much care and attention as if she'd made them herself. Seeing him enter, her wide, spontaneous smile lit her whole face and hit him like a sucker punch. She may have turned down his dinner invitation, but she wasn't sorry to see him again.

"Did you forget something?" she asked.

"I want to buy a gift. Gloves or a scarf or something."

"A gift for your girlfriend…or wife?" she murmured.

Normally he hated it when people blatantly fished for information about his private life. In his previous career as a professional hockey player, he'd had his share of sports groupies so he didn't blame Tina for checking. If she even knew who he was, that is. But he was putting the moves on her. The fact she was asking suggested she was interested.

"No wife. No girlfriend." If he didn't have such a jaundiced view of marriage thanks to his parents' dysfunctional union he might have gotten hitched by now. Instead, he was more about having fun than settling down. Why the hell not? Life was short. Mistakes in choosing a partner lasted a lifetime. Or at least until divorce. "What about you?" he said.

"No. No wife or girlfriend either," she said, smiling mischievously. "No, Luke. I am single too. So then, who do you buy this gift for?"

His pulse quickened knowing she was available. "My sister's birthday is coming up."

"How about a scarf?" Tina moved behind the glass cabinet that showcased neatly folded silk scarves. "What color are her eyes?"

"Brown."

"What kind of an answer is that? Light brown, dark brown, hazel?"

"Um…" He was so distracted by her voluptuous curves, her musical accent, the way she carved the air with her hands as she spoke, that it took him a moment to picture Stella. "Sort of medium."

"Lighter than mine, or darker?"

"Let me look." He reached across the counter and tipped her chin. Tina's eyes were large and wide set, slightly tilted up at the corners and fringed by thick black lashes. The color of her irises was a clear, rich amber with tiny flecks of dark brown around the edge. Was there even a name for that color? There ought to be. They were like jewels. Her pupils dilated and a rosy glow appeared on her smooth, olive-toned cheekbones.

Her lips parted slightly. "Well?"

"Stella's are lighter brown, with a bit of green. More like hazel I guess." His voice had gone all gravelly. He eased back to glance around. "Like that dress, the one on the left in the window with the pleats up top."

"I know just the thing." Tina slid out a drawer from under the glass-topped counter and sifted through neatly folded scarves. She unfurled a wide square of silk in autumn hues, the predominant color a rich mossy green, like the creek that used to run through the woods near their small upstate town when they were kids. "Would this suit her?"

"Yes," he said, surprised at how accurate her guess was. "It looks like something she would choose herself." If Stella had the bucks to buy anything remotely as expensive as an article from a Madison Avenue boutique, that is. Any extra money she had went to care for her disabled son, Timmy. He helped with that too. As much as she'd allow him.

"I'll wrap it up." Tina folded the scarf expertly back into the box and took it to the counter. Crouching, she hunted through one cabinet after another. "Sorry, we're not even really open yet. Ah, here it is." She brought out gift wrap and ribbon.

Luke brought out his leather wallet from his back pocket and pulled out a platinum credit card. "How much do I owe you?"

Tina made a scoffing sound and waved a hand. "Don't even think about paying after all the help you've given me today."

"That was freely given. Of course I'll pay. I don't want

you out of pocket." Tina opened her mouth, no doubt to protest, but he cut her off. "Don't tell me it's not a problem, because I know what it's like to be on a limited income." A long time ago for him, but those days of childhood poverty had left their mark. "How much?"

"I'm serious. It's on the house." Tina clipped off the price tag and tossed it away before he could grab it and look.

"Your boss isn't going to be happy."

"She won't mind when I tell her how much you helped me. The real handyman didn't even show up. If you hadn't come along, the boutique would be in trouble." She expertly wrapped the present and taped the ends shut. Her eyes danced merrily as she presented him with the gift.

Luke was stumped. He literally had no clue what a designer scarf would be worth. When he'd been a hockey player his manager had taken care of presents for whatever woman he was dating at the time, and all the bills went to his accountant. But given the upscale nature of the boutique... He put away his credit card and plunked down a handful of hundred dollar bills. "You're taking the money. No arguments."

Tina opened her mouth as if to protest. He threw her a warning look. She shrugged and opened the cash register. "Okay, you win."

He picked up the slim wrapped package. "Have you changed your mind about dinner?"

"I'm sorry, I can't. I'm embarrassed to admit it, but I'm exhausted." Sure enough, she had to cover a huge yawn with her hand. "And there's that early morning."

"We don't have to make it a late night." In case she was wavering, he stepped up the charm offensive with his best smile. "We could go to bed real early."

Her hands went uncharacteristically still. They were small and neat, with clear nail polish. Her only jewelry was a thin gold chain around her wrist and a delicate gold ring set with a small ruby. It was probably fake, but it was pretty enough.

"I was joking about bed." Unless she liked the idea.

She raised cloudy eyes to his. "Why did you kiss me earlier?"

Huh? Did she even have to ask? If ever there was a no brainer… "You're beautiful. I couldn't help myself." He shifted uneasily. "Look, if I offended you, I'm sorry."

A curious expression crossed her oval face, part wistful, part uncertain, part…angry? Her emotions were so volatile, so close to the surface, it was hard to know what was coming next.

"So you think I'm sexy even though I'm just a sales girl?"

Just a sales girl? Where did that come from? "Who cares what you do for a living? Who you are as a person is more important. I've barely been able to keep my hands off you all afternoon."

"I…have a confession to make, too," she said.

"Yeah?" Spotting a tiny fleck of sugar on her cheek from the pastry she'd eaten earlier he leaned forward and licked it off with the tip of his tongue. Beautiful and *delicious*. His groin stirred. He nuzzled her cheek, breathing in the scent of her skin. "What is it? Something naughty, I hope."

"I…" she began then paused a beat. And another.

"Go on," he encouraged in a deliberately suggestive tone as he ran a finger just under the neckline of her dress. Her skin was unbelievably soft and warm. "What kind of kinkiness are you going to admit to?"

Her throaty laugh made him think maybe he wasn't too far off the mark. He was positively intrigued, his mind conjuring a dozen scenarios, each one hotter than the next. He arched a brow, daring her to tell him.

She caught her bottom lip between her teeth. Tugging on a springy lock of dark hair, she shot him an enigmatic glance. "Not that I've ever done it before but sometimes I think it would be fun to pretend to be I'm someone I'm not."

Interesting, but that didn't tell him enough. "What do you mean?"

"You know, to escape reality just for a little while. Be someone different." From the way her eyes batted up at him, all big and innocent in her pretty face, he got the impression this wasn't something she normally shared. She crossed her arms, suddenly shy and uncertain.

He scratched his head and tried to lighten the mood. "Well…I'm happy being me. But I do a pretty good impression of a pirate king." He didn't normally go for lame-ass voiceovers, but she looked so lost and earnest. "Would you care to hear it?"

Her entire face brightened, and in that moment, he probably would've walked a plank to see that smile. "Avast me hearties," he teased. "Take this wench to my cabin for immediate ravishing." He leaned in and winked. "Wait till you see my cutlass."

She rolled her eyes, but they were sparkling again. "I'm sure it's very impressive."

"So you'll come out with me tonight?"

"You're very tempting, but I'm not dating. I need to focus on my work."

As a brush off, that was right up there with "I need to wash my hair." Had he read her wrong, only imagined the chemistry between them? Maybe she was simply a warm, expressive, naturally affectionate person who responded to everyone the way she'd had with him.

Nah. He was no Einstein, but he wasn't stupid. He knew women. A very physical and compelling vibe was bouncing back and forth between them. He hadn't come looking for it, and it wasn't exactly convenient given how busy he was with the bar and his children's foundation, not to mention coaching the disabled kids' hockey team. But he couldn't walk away.

On the other hand, he wasn't a guy who thought women really meant yes when they said no. If she had reservations she didn't want to tell him about, he wasn't going to pressure her.

"All right. But if you change your mind, you've got my card. If you need anything at all, give me a call."

"*Si, va bene*." She came around the counter and linked her arm with his as naturally as if they were old friends—or new lovers—and walked him to the door. "Once again, *ciao*, and thank you for your help. And for…everything."

"I'll see you soon, I hope. Tina—"

"You must go now." She closed the door slowly, pushing him out.

He poked his head back inside. "Was the pirate schtick too corny? I'll try something else. Remember, I can be anyone you want me to be."

For a second, she wavered, her luminous eyes glazing over as if she was fantasizing about the possibilities.

"You like cowboys?" he went on. "I do a mean John

Wayne impression."

She snapped out of it. "*Ciao*," she said firmly, laughing, and shut the door.

Twice. She'd turned him down twice. He, Luke Pedersen, hailed as the greatest player since Wayne Gretsky. He couldn't recall the last time he'd been rejected by a woman. His sister would probably say it was character-building for him to be taken down a peg. But it sucked.

What's more, he couldn't recall the last time he'd been so attracted to a woman. And it wasn't just her looks, although the little Italian next door had a body that wouldn't quit. There'd been passion and pride and something he couldn't quite name in her big, beautiful eyes. There was just something about *her*. It intrigued him. He wouldn't beg — and, shit, he'd come damn close to doing just that — but he wanted to see her again. It dawned on him that he *would* see her again, likely every day, with her now working right next door. She'd come around. With that thought, he whistled as he strolled through Hat Trick's front door.

At the bar, he quickly settled back to work, replacing the skirting board in the kitchen where he'd had new ovens, sinks and stainless steel cabinets installed. With a practiced hand, he hammered home the nails with a couple of taps. The electrician was finishing up the wiring, and the plasterer was patching up behind him. Luke didn't mind pitching in. Before he'd turned pro and started getting fat contracts, he'd worked construction in small towns all over the upstate area.

While he worked, his thoughts kept returning to Tina. She was a whirlwind of energy, constantly on the move, hands gesturing, eyes lighting up like a scoreboard, broadcasting her every emotion. He'd love to see her with her hair down.

His fingers had itched to pull out the clip holding up the thick, curling mass. And her Italian accent was incredibly sexy. Combined with her sultry voice—wow.

If his old teammates could have seen him carrying mannequins in a ladies' boutique, they would have laughed him off the ice. But Tina had that kind of power to make a guy want to do anything for her.

He wondered what she'd been thinking when she'd grabbed hold of his tool belt to get his tape measure. And how did she manage to smell sweet and spicy at the same time? When she was up on the ladder, with the smooth olive skin of her calf at eye level, he'd wanted to nibble and lick his way up to the back of her knee. And higher….

Whoa, he needed to put a lid on it. He would—he promised himself he would—but there was just something so intriguing about the woman. Something he couldn't puzzle out. Between his childhood dealing with his mother's bullshit, the years on the ice facing-off with opponents, and the time since spent in the bar, he'd become something of an expert at quickly reading people. And something about Tina didn't add up.

What was her story? She didn't seem like the type to play hard to get. More like a woman who went after what she wanted. Yet despite her fiery, bossy temperament there'd been moments when she'd seemed vulnerable, almost fragile. How could she even ask if he thought she was sexy? Had someone hurt her, badly enough to make her wary? If so, he'd gladly pummel the bastard.

"What does a guy have to do to get a beer around here?" a voice called over the whine of power drills and hammering.

"Sorry, we're not open—" Luke emerged from the back

to see his old friend and financial advisor, Allan Montes. "Al, buddy. What the hell are you doing so far from Wall Street?"

"I've been trying to call you." Allan, with his fancy suit and three hundred dollar haircut, slid onto a stool. Geeze, the man's hair was as polished as the mahogany bar. When Luke and his teammates had been in the race for the Cup, they'd go weeks without shaving, let alone getting haircuts. But athletes were funny like that, bending to superstitions and dedicated to odd rituals. He ran a hand over his smooth jaw. Those days were long gone but they still made him smile.

"Guess you couldn't hear your cell over all this noise," Allan said. "What the hell are you doing, anyway? As if the bar and the foundation aren't enough for you, now you're moonlighting as a carpenter?"

"I want the kitchen finished so I can reopen tomorrow." Luke picked up his cell phone from under the counter. "I forgot this here while I was next door at the boutique."

He checked his log and sure enough Allan had left a couple of messages. There was one from his mother too. His jaw tightened as he hit delete. It had been a while since she'd called begging for money, but he wasn't convinced her life-long gambling problem was miraculously cured. It hurt like hell that he couldn't trust his own mother to tell the truth, but he—and his whole family—had been burned too many times.

"Boutique?" Allan's eyebrows rose as he shook a handful of peanuts from the glass carafe on the bar into his hand. "Got a new girlfriend?"

"Nope." Luke took a couple of long necks out of the fridge, cracked them open and slid one across the bar. "I was helping the sales assistant with some heavy lifting."

"Was she hot?" Allan tossed a peanut in his mouth.

"She was all right." He and Allan had spent many a night clubbing together and sharing stories of the women they hooked up with. But right now his friend's salacious tone grated. "What brings you to my den of iniquity so early in the evening?"

"Bad news, that's what." Allan wiped his hands on a bev nap and reached for his briefcase. He opened it to take out a manila envelope. "I've been doing the yearly audit of the foundation."

"Oh?" He didn't like the ominous set to Allan's jaw. Luke had founded the Disabled Children's Sports Foundation after he'd retired from the Rangers. What had started as a tax shelter quickly became something much more. First he'd taught Stella's little boy, Timmy, who was in a wheel chair, to skate. Then he'd gotten more disabled kids involved and started coaching. Now his disabled kids' hockey team and the foundation that supported it were the most important things in his life after his family. He poured most of his spare cash, time, and energy into the charity. "Give it to me straight."

"Bottom line—you're up shit creek." Allan tossed a summary sheet across the bar. "The board bought what they thought was an amazeballs financial product that the bank was pushing like crack cocaine. Turns out it was mostly junk bonds. Now the market's falling, and the bank is calling in the bonds, but they're worthless. The directors tried to 'fix' the situation by selling other, blue chip stocks to pay for it, hoping to get back on an even keel. But it was too little, too late. The foundation is tapped out and left owing a big chunk of change."

"*What?*" Luke shook his head. The board of directors were all solid businessmen. Or so he'd thought. This couldn't be real. "When did all this happen? *How* could it happen? Why didn't they check into the investments more closely?"

"Happened months ago. The board kept it quiet, hoping to get out of hot water," Allan said. "The people who put these financial products together are unscrupulous and good at hiding the bad elements. The board probably knew they were taking a risk but your mission statement is to expand so they took a chance. Unfortunately for all concerned it turned to shit."

A sinkhole opened up in Luke's stomach. "Fuck."

"Precisely."

"What does this mean for the kids?"

Allan's mouth thinned to a grim line. "Unless you find five million dollars in the next week you'll have to severely curtail the programs. There's very little money left for operating costs and forget about expanding."

Luke swore again and kicked a plastic crate out of his way. He could put expanding the Foundation's reach on hold but to cut the existing program? Hell, no. "They've got games lined up. They've been practicing so hard." And not just the hockey team he coached but all the other programs for disabled kids, some of whom were playing sports for the first time in their lives. There were chapters in ten cities on the eastern seaboard and they were growing all the time.

Allan shrugged unhappily. "We'll talk to the bank, ask them to extend a line of credit until—"

"Until what?" Luke set his beer bottle down hard. "I'm not going to get another multi-million dollar hockey contract. The bar pays its own way and makes a tidy profit but it doesn't bring in enough revenue to support the foundation." All he could think of was the disappointment on the kids' faces if he had to tell them they couldn't play hockey anymore.

"We had practice this morning," he told Allan. "Those kids are so gutsy. You should see Timmy zipping around the ice in his wheel chair like he's driving Formula One. We'll make the playoffs if we win our game this week. If there is another game, that is." His fist tightened on his beer bottle. "I need to raise money, fast."

Allan sighed. "You could sell some property. Those houses you bought for your parents and your sister and brother. Together they're worth nearly five mill."

Luke was shaking his head before Allan even finished. "Forget it. Those were gifts. No way would I ever ask for them back."

"I didn't think so." Allan paused. "The bar then? With a deed of sale the bank would likely give you a couple months leeway while it's in escrow. It won't be enough, but it might buy you a little time."

The bar provided income that supplemented his family's households. 'Cause sure as shit, he might have bought them million dollar homes, but that didn't mean they could afford the taxes and insurance and utilities on them. Then there was the extra his mom needed every month after she poured her grocery money down the slot machines the way she'd done ever since he could remember. She hadn't done it for months, but that could just mean she'd found some other sucker to support her habits. He wondered briefly if he should've called her back, and then pushed the thought aside. She'd made her choices; the disabled kids his foundation supported…they never had a choice.

"I could sell my apartment," Luke said. "It's worth a bundle."

"And then where are you going to live?" Allan demanded. "You love that place."

"I'll find something smaller. It's no big deal. The clock is ticking. Nothing means as much to me as the foundation." It was the simple truth. He'd been coaching the same bunch of boys for two years now, and while Timmy was naturally his favorite being his nephew, he loved them all. He knew about their individual challenges and their families and how hard it was for many of them to cope. Hockey was the bright spot in their lives. It was his, too.

"You do realize that I can't, as your advisor, recommend that you compromise your life or your investments for this. Right?"

Luke frowned. "I don't expect you to understand—"

"I've seen you with those kids. I get it. Hell, I'd make a sizable donation if I thought it would help. But this isn't salvageable, Luke. It's five million dollars. It can take years to raise that much money for any organization—"

"I'm not letting it fail. I won't." Too many kids depended on it. For so many of them, it was their only break, their only escape from the world.

"You're not going to help them much if you end up sleeping under a bridge," Allan said. "Don't do anything rash."

The operating expenses for the programs he'd established were huge. Rink time, transportation, equipment, custom prosthetics and physical therapists… The kids literally got the best support the foundation could offer. Then there were the doctors' bills that were supplemented. He knew how costly treatments were for children with disabilities, and he had families depending on the support that his foundation provided. With dozens of teams and almost two hundred kids relying on him, there was no way he could let his foundation fold.

Frustrated, Luke paced some more. At times like this he wished he could lace on his skates and take to the ice—feel the cold air on his face as he raced around the rink, hear the crack of wood on puck as he sunk a slap shot. He stopped abruptly. "That's it! I've got it. An exhibition game. Rangers versus Islanders, all proceeds to the foundation."

"Okay, now you're talking." He could practically see Allan calculating the ticket price by the number of seats in Madison Square Garden. "That's a great idea." Allan raised his bottle in salute.

"I'll call the guys. I know they'll be glad to help." Luke's brain was firing on all cylinders now. "I'll go on the Mike & Mike show to publicize the game. Ask for donations. Viewers can call in and contribute."

"I'll talk to the bank and see if they'll extend a line of credit." Allan shut his briefcase and gave Luke a brisk man-hug. "This situation really sucks. But if anyone can pull a rabbit out of the hat, it's you."

Luke walked him to the door. He felt better just having a plan of action. "I'm no magician. But I'm going to find a way to make it work."

Chapter Three

Tina nodded at the uniformed doorman as she entered the opulent lobby of the St. Regis Hotel. Her feet ached from being on them all day and jet lag had her dragging said-aching feet across the marble foyer. She was looking forward to room service, a shower and an early night.

Really? Then why did she regret turning down Luke's invitation to dinner? Half a dozen times during the day she'd been tempted to run next door and tell him yes, she would love to go out with him. Unfortunately, logic and good sense had won out over her attraction. Men simply couldn't be trusted, not when their own self-interest was at stake. Oh, she had no reason to distrust Luke. He seemed like a perfectly nice guy. Well, maybe *nice* was too tame a word for the brawny bar owner. But she'd been fooled before, so thoroughly it had shaken her. Even more than she didn't trust men, she didn't trust her own judgment.

On her way to the elevator, she stopped in the hotel

convenience store for headache tablets. Fabio's photo on the cover of a *Marie Claire* magazine in the rack next to the checkout caught her eye. His arm was around a blonde with acres of tanned skin and a very skimpy bikini as the couple posed on a yacht moored in Monaco. In the background was the very hotel where she'd met him at a fashion shoot. If she looked closely she could even see the window of the suite on the third floor where they'd first made love.

Tina flipped to the story inside. The blonde was a famous model and a member of the British aristocracy who had her own line of cosmetics. *Of course she did.* There was a brief mention of Fabio's court case with Tina but it was glossed over as a minor financial dispute with an irate former girlfriend.

A slow burn made her want to crumple the magazine and throw against the wall. He didn't deserve to be out having fun, conning another gullible woman into giving him money. How he'd gotten away without a conviction she couldn't fathom. All the time he swore he loved her, he'd been siphoning off the funds she'd given him for a photography studio — with her name on the deed as a co-owner — into a private bank account in the Bahamas. Fabio had committed the crime but Tina was the one suffering. That wasn't right. It wasn't fair.

And he'd had the nerve to complain about her weight when *he* was the cause of her need for sugary, comfort food. She scowled at his smirking photograph. The asshole had deliberately tried to make her feel bad about herself. She wished she had a *bombolone*. The custard-filled donut would go down really well right now.

She put the magazine back on the rack, muttering to the

blonde, "Good luck, *bella*. You're going to need it."

Suddenly the thought of stewing over Fabio alone in her hotel room was intolerable. Especially when she could have spent the evening with Luke, a handsome, sexy man who wanted her for who she was, not what she could do for him. A man who had come to her aid when she needed help. Why had she said no? She deserved to enjoy herself, didn't she? Was she really going to let her ex stop her from being open to seeing other men? That was only hurting her. She truly, honestly, didn't care about him anymore so why did she care if he was out there having a good time? Let him. Someday karma would have him twisting in the wind where he belonged.

Tina rummaged through her purse and found Luke's card. She tapped it against her palm, some of her doubts and fears seeping back in. What did she really know about him? He'd tried to fool her briefly into thinking he was a handy-man. On the other hand, he'd told her the truth before he left, and he had nothing to gain. He'd kept up the ruse so he could spend time with her. She was flattered. *He* made her feel good about herself. As she should.

Bottom line, she really wanted to see him. Before she could second-guess herself any further, she found a quiet corner of the lobby and punched in his number.

"Hello?" he answered on the second ring, sounding impatient or frustrated. Maybe even angry.

She wondered what the rest of his life was like. Running a bar must have its own set of challenges. Too many drunks, not enough customers…? Whatever it was that bothered him, maybe they could take each other's minds off their problems.

In the boutique, he'd teased her about pretending to be someone else, and hearing him laugh had been the bright spot of her whole day. Perhaps she could return the favor.

"Hey, cowboy," she drawled. "It's Tina, from the boutique." She did her best to mimic a western accent. Spaghetti western, maybe. It must sound silly with her Italian accent. But when she was in Rome, being Bettina Borlenghi, head of a famous atelier, she never got to act silly. This was fun. "Do you still want to," –what was the term? "How do you say, chow down with me?"

His deep laugh rumbled in her ear. "Well now, I reckon I do, little lady," he said in a passable imitation of John Wayne. She could almost see him tip an imaginary ten-gallon hat. "Where and when should I pick you up?"

"Meet me at the boutique in half an hour." She forgot to put on an accent and her words came out in a rush. "We'll go somewhere from there." Taking a breath, she added, "Don't be late. I am hungry."

"I'll be there. On the dot."

Tina hung up and headed for the elevator, her mind already racing ahead to the clothes she'd packed. She was tempted to wear something cowgirl-like. Oh yes, if she was going to take him up on his offer, then she'd go all-in. Fantasy, fun, her deepest desires—she wanted it all.

But in the end, she played it safe and chose an outfit that was classy but sexy. For the first time in many months, she was looking forward to going out, hooking up with an exciting man. A man who didn't know her but who liked her.

Her reflection in the mirrored wall of the elevator gazed back at her accusingly. What about her, letting him think she was a salesgirl? Well, she had her reasons, and she meant no harm. She hated lying even by omission, but she felt compelled to hide her identity. It wasn't as if they were getting involved in a relationship. It was only a flirtation with no strings attached. He didn't need to know everything about her, and vice versa.

For years now, she'd been in the spotlight as one of the heirs of the Borlenghi fortune, a target for men from London to Tokyo. Even before Fabio, she'd never quite been certain if a man was with her for her own sake or because she had connections and money. Oh, she believed she was attractive enough, inside and out, to be worthy of attention. But she'd been so sure Fabio had loved her. And she'd been so wrong. Now with every new man there would always be that tiny niggling doubt.

Surely just this once she could remain anonymous and know that if Luke kissed her it was because he thought she was desirable in her own right, not because he could get something from her. If that was a rationalization, so be it.

• • •

At five minutes to seven, Luke leaned against the marble column outside the Borlenghi Boutique, twirling the stem of a big, red, daisy-like flower he'd bought after reading Tina's text message saying she'd be a few minutes late. At ten past seven, he glimpsed her on the crowded sidewalk and stuffed his phone in the front pocket of his jeans.

Waves of her abundant dark hair cascaded down her back, bouncing lightly as her high heels clicked briskly along the concrete. Men's heads turned as she passed. And why not? Her full breasts were molded by a sleeveless scarlet top that exposed a sliver of tanned midriff. A leather skirt curved over her flaring hips and stopped enticingly just above her knees. Luke's imagination ran wild wondering what lay underneath.

A smile lit her face when she caught sight of him. He straightened as she checked him out from his button down shirt to his black jeans. Then her smiled turned amused when her gaze landed on the pair of lovingly-polished cowboy boots he'd bought years ago in Dallas. She brought out the playful side of him. "Hey, Cowboy, is that a phone in your pocket or are you just glad to see me?"

"Howdy, ma'am. Fastest texter in the Upper West." He whipped it out as if it was a gun and sent her a message.

She swiped her phone open and read aloud, "*You make my six shooter go bang*."

Her knowing smile and sexy accent sent his blood south, and Luke felt his groin tighten, imagining her talking dirty in Italian. He handed her the flower and gave her a lingering, but chaste, kiss on the mouth. An appetizer of things to come. She smelled sultry and spicy, like a balmy night on the Amalfi coast.

"*Grazie*." She broke off the end of the flower stem and tucked the red bloom into her flowing dark hair. "What are we going to eat?"

"Cowboys eat hot dogs and beans," he deadpanned then laughed at her surprised expression. "Hardly. I know a great Argentinian restaurant. "

"Wonderful. I'm so hungry I could eat a whole cow." She glanced at Hat Trick where a group of young hipsters were entering. "Do you serve food?"

"Just tapas. Not very satisfying for a starving cowgirl."

He was proud of his bar but he didn't want to take her where everyone knew him and fifty other guys would be ogling his date. Some place more romantic would be better. He hailed a taxi.

"I love asado," Tina said. "Last year in Buenos Aires—" She broke off abruptly, biting her bottom lip.

She often started sentences she didn't finish, he'd noticed. "Go on." The cab pulled in to the curb and Luke opened the door for her. "Have you been to Argentina?"

She gave a nervous laugh as she got in. "No, I meant an Argentinian restaurant named Buenos Aires."

"Ah." Of course. She probably couldn't afford to travel. He hoped he hadn't embarrassed her. "Whereabouts in Manhattan is it? Do you want to go there now?"

She bent to adjust the strap on her high heeled sandal. "I…no, I think it closed down."

"We'll hit the one I know then." Luke gave the driver an address. He'd called Andres, the owner, earlier. The restaurateur was a big hockey fan and had promised Luke a prime table for two.

"You must have influence to get in on short notice," Tina said. "Normally you can't walk in off the street at a top restaurant unless you know someone or you're famous. At least, I imagine you can't."

"Oh, well, restaurants, bars, we're all friends in the business." And because it troubled him that he could still hear Tina's whispered voice saying, "You lied to me" he added, "I used to play ice hockey. I was fairly well known."

"You were famous? What is your full name?"

"Luke Pederson." He chuckled at her blank look. "I take it you're not a hockey fan."

"I like football. What you call soccer. My brother owns—" Again she stumbled over her words. "He owns…much memorabilia. He has a football signed by all the members of the Naples team."

"Cool. Does your brother still live in Italy?"

"*Sì.*" Her hand rose to tug on a long curling lock.

Damn, he'd made her uncomfortable again. Luke took her hand and pulled it away from her hair to fold it in his own. "You must miss him. How long since you've been home?"

"Not so long." She turned to look out the window at the shops as the taxi wove in and out of traffic down Lexington Avenue.

With her gaze averted Luke was free to study her. Her fine leather skirt and well-cut top were trendy, but they didn't look cheap. Probably working in the fashion industry she got designer clothing deeply discounted. But unless he was mistaken, those sparklers at her ears and around her throat were real diamonds. Were they a present, maybe from a man? Well that wouldn't be surprising, would it? She was stunning, an incredibly desirable woman. A twinge of jealousy pricked him unexpectedly. He'd only just met the woman and already he didn't like the thought of her with other men, even in the past. Even though he wasn't looking for anything as serious as a relationship.

When they arrived at the restaurant, it was just as he remembered, colorful and noisy, the atmosphere thick with the mouth-watering aroma of charring meats. Luke set aside his uneasy ruminations and greeted Andres with a handshake and a clap on the back. "Thanks for fitting us in."

"Anytime, *amigo.*" Andres bowed his dark head over Tina's hand. "*Buenas noches, Señorita.*" To Luke's surprise,

Tina returned the greeting and added a few more words in perfect Spanish.

Andres showed them to their table personally. "Enjoy your meal."

"Come by the bar sometime so I can return the favor." When he left, Luke turned to Tina. "You speak Spanish too?"

"It's similar to Italian."

Okay, that was certainly true. The waiter brought menus and a bowl of marinated olives to start. "So, how long have you lived in New York?"

Tina hesitated, twisting the stem of her wineglass. "Not long."

"How long is 'not long?'"

She pushed her glass away and met his gaze directly. "I don't actually live in New York. I'm only here to help with the launch of the boutique and for fashion week. I...I work for the company in Italy."

"Oh." That made a few things click into place. It was an unwelcome bit of news that took him a moment to process. He realized he'd been looking forward to having her as a permanent feature in the boutique next to his sports bar. "So you're here for a good time, not a long time."

"I am." Amber eyes sparkling, she leaned toward him, showing a glimpse of awesome cleavage. "When time is short, it's important not to waste it."

Every cloud had a silver lining. If she wasn't sticking around then she wouldn't have any expectations of him. Win-win. He covered her hand, gently squeezing. "It almost seems a shame to spend it eating."

"Oh, don't say that. Eating is a pure pleasure." She

turned her hand over so their palms and fingertips pressed together. "Like sex."

Luke wasn't often at a loss for words but the way she said "sex" in that husky voice was enough to close his throat and send his blood coursing south. While he was still struggling for control, she chose an olive with slender fingers and sunk her white teeth into the juicy brown skin. Mesmerized, he watched her lush crimson mouth move as she chewed.

Tina wiped her fingers on a napkin. She gave him a challenging, sultry glance. "So you like being bossed around."

Oh, yeah. A week with her would be better than a month with a lesser woman. His foot found hers beneath the table, and he slid his ankle next to hers. "Sometimes. Mostly I like to do the bossing."

"When two strong personalities collide…" Tina slid her hand out from under his, but slowly, so it seemed more of a caress than a withdrawal, and then clapped suddenly. "Kaboom!"

"I like explosions. Big fan of fireworks." He would have continued with the pyrotechnics theme but he noticed the waiter hovering nearby. "Do you know what you want?"

Her smile deepened. "Oh, yes, I know exactly what I want."

"Stop it." He laughed even as his body tightened. Very strange feeling to be amused and turned on at the same time. "Or we'll never get to dessert."

"Okay, I'll be good." She turned to the waiter and rattled off her order in fluent Spanish, eliciting near adoration in the young server.

"I'll have what she's having," Luke said, then turned back to Tina, who was perusing the wine list. He nudged her leg. "See anything you like?"

She glanced up at him beneath her lashes, conveying the message without a word—she liked what she saw across the table. "You choose."

Luke scanned the wine list. "The 1988 Temperanillo," he said to the waiter then turned back to Tina. Did she like dressing up and playing sexy roles or had he misconstrued her earlier comments? He'd love to find out. He could easily picture her in a cowboy hat and nothing else. "So, l'il lady," he said, reverting to John Wayne. "Tell me about your life in Italy."

"As I said, I live in Rome. But I spent much of my childhood in Naples. We still go there a lot, to the family y—" She broke off abruptly.

"Y—?" he repeated. "The family yurt? Yellow submarine? Yak?"

"My grandparents live there," she said, not answering the question. "Have you been to Italy?"

"I've been to the Amalfi Coast and Capri. I was in Venice a few years ago for a film festival. My girlfriend at the time was an actress nominated for an award. She didn't win but it was good 'exposure' as she put it."

"Exposure can be overrated." Tina shuddered delicately. Then she paused. "You're not with her now?"

He shook his head. "I enjoyed your country though. And the Italians I met."

"Italy is very different from America. We don't have such a thing as a sports bar, for instance. Watching TV in public while you eat and drink…it's unthinkable."

"What do you do instead then?"

"We talk to each other." Her ankle had remained

pressed next to his since he'd found her under the table. Now she slipped her foot out of her shoe and ran her toes up his calf. "Conversation is the sincerest form of foreplay, don't you think?"

His pants became painfully tight. If this kept up he would go "kaboom" as she put it before they made it through the appetizers. "Absolutely. I could...*talk*...for hours."

The waiter came back with the wine. Luke knew all the right things to do, swirling and examining the color, sniffing the scent and finally letting a sip roll around in his mouth. It wasn't craft beer but it was pretty damn good just the same. He nodded his approval and the wine was poured.

Luke clinked glasses with Tina. "*Salute.*"

Her glorious smile lit her face at his knowing the Italian for "cheers." "Now, where were we?"

He leaned back in his chair but let his ankle rub against hers beneath the table. He needed to settle down, pace himself. Sex with a woman as beautiful and interesting as Tina, like a fabulous meal, deserved to savored. "I believe we were...conversing."

Chapter Four

"*Bellissimo*." Tina stepped into Luke's living room, immediately charmed by the warm green walls, comfortable leather furniture and polished wood coffee and end tables. Mood lighting filled the room with a soft glow and piano music tinkled from unseen speakers. "Very cozy."

"Cozy?" Luke laughed. "I don't like to brag but twenty-four hundred square feet is a mansion in New York terms."

She wondered what he would make of her half-acre villa in Rome or her four-story house in the heart of Paris. Luckily he had no idea. "I only meant that despite how large and grand this room, you've managed to make it warm and comfortable."

"Thanks, I like it." He moved into the kitchen. "Wine? Beer? Champagne?"

"Champagne, *grazie*—" Tina broke off, her eye caught by the painting over the fireplace. "My God, can it be?" She moved to examine more closely the painting of a young boy in a dark forest and to check the signature. Her hand went to her cheek and she shook her head in awe. "It is."

"Is what?" Luke asked. In the kitchen a cork popped.

"A Hurstbridge. I had no idea there was a second one. Do you know there's a matching painting of a young girl, also in the woods?"

She knew because she owned the other painting, bought last year when she'd come to New York to find a location for her boutique. It was an amazing coincidence. She had to bite her lip to stop herself from telling Luke about her painting. He would never believe a sales assistant could buy such expensive artwork.

"I had no idea." He handed her a glass of sparkling wine and stood close, his arm brushing her shoulder. "Are the paintings similar?"

"Very." She sipped her champagne. Mm, Dom, nice. Luke had good taste. "Same woods, same brooding atmosphere. The artist evokes so much emotion."

"I picked this up at an auction in SoHo a few years back. At first glance, I thought it was full of foreboding and sadness. Why is the boy all alone? Is he safe? Where are his parents? Then I looked at it a while longer and it seemed more like he's on a quest. Where is he going? Will he get there before darkness falls? Is he traveling to meet someone?"

"*Sì!*" She touched his arm, excited that he had the same reaction as she did. "At first you think, poor *bambino*. And then you look closer and get the sense he has a purpose. A mission."

"Exactly. See the shaft of light in the upper right hand corner? I like to think that represents hope." Luke put his arm around her neck and pointed to a faint gleam coming from a source outside the frame. His cheek was almost touching hers. "Which way is the girl walking? Same direction?"

"No, she faces the opposite direction." Tina turned to him with a brilliant smile. "Maybe they're traveling through the woods toward each other."

"It sounds as if the pictures are meant to belong together," Luke said. "Where did you see the girl painting? I'd like to buy it."

"I… In a gallery somewhere. I can't remember." Oh dear, this line of conversation could get awkward. She glanced around, searching for a change of topic, and picked up the first thing at hand from the mantelpiece, a trophy. "What's this for?"

"I coach hockey for disabled kids. My nephew Timmy is on the team. He…" Luke paused, cleared his throat and went on. "He was crazy excited last year when we won the division final and got this trophy. Meant so much to him, and all the kids."

"It sounds like it means a lot to you too."

"Most important thing I've ever done," he said gruffly. "When my sister Stella asked me to teach Timmy to play hockey the poor kid hardly had any friends, very little exercise and almost no fun. Now he's like a different kid, always joking around."

"You've done something very special for those children," Tina said.

"In many ways, coaching has helped me as much as I've helped the kids, keeping me in touch with the sport I love. But it's not about me. The kids have come out of their shells. Hockey gives them something to focus on besides their disabilities. A goal to strive for. It boosts their self-esteem and improves their general health. Don't know what they—or I—will do if we have to give it up."

Tina touched his arm. "Why would you have to? I don't understand."

"Oh, it's nothing, just a cash flow problem threatening the program. I've got some fundraising ideas on the go. It'll all work out." Casually he took the trophy from her and replaced it on the mantelpiece, but the lines between his eyebrows had deepened.

Clearly it wasn't "nothing." And even though the words "cash flow problem" were enough to set the alarm bells clanging in her head, she couldn't ignore children in need. Or that this was about Luke's family. "What can I can do to help?"

He touched her cheek. "It's good of you to offer, but I've got it under control."

"At least let me know where I can make a donation." It was on the tip of her tongue to ask if she could see the children play a game, but she pulled back. She and Luke weren't in a relationship. For as intense as this strange attraction was, they'd only just met.

"When the collection site is in place, I'll let you know."

"Promise?" He nodded but naturally he wouldn't believe her capable of making a large enough contribution to make a difference. It was frustrating not to be able to tell him who she was. She really should clear up the whole misunderstanding before it reached the point that admitting the truth would be too embarrassing.

But she wasn't ready to let go of that sexy gleam in Luke's eyes when he flirted with her. Telling him she was the head of a large fashion design house would change the way he acted around her, guaranteed. Fabio might be the only man who had used her so badly, but most people treated her differently because of her heritage.

"To get back to what we were talking about, you said you haven't been in New York long," he said, bringing them back to the previous topic. "So you must have seen the girl painting recently."

"I really can't remember where. I was just walking around. I don't even know the area." Was it her imagination or was he watching her closely? It was harder than she'd thought to pretend to be someone she wasn't. But then, she wasn't used to lying. To escape his scrutiny, she strolled away from the fireplace, sipping her drink.

Luke followed. "Champagne all right?"

"Dom is my favorite." She spun to him and with her free hand, ran her fingertips along the collar of his shirt. She undid the top button. And the next. Beneath the fine cotton, his skin was warm and alive. She swayed closer, breathing in his aftershave, spicy and seductive. "You're spoiling me."

"Dom Perignon is your favorite champagne?" His eyebrows rose, and she could hear the wonder in his voice. "You're full of surprises."

She eased away again, kicking herself for being too distracted by his nearness to make up another, cheaper brand. Why did she have to name it at all? "At fashion week in Paris and Rome there is lots of free food and drink." Only the elite inner circle drank the good stuff and she was usually the one supplying it, but he didn't need to know that. "I confess I've developed champagne tastes."

Again, he closed the gap between them, reminding her of a big cat on the prowl. "Ah, finally we have your confession."

She quirked an eyebrow at him over the rim of her flute. "And you didn't even have to torture me to get it."

"Damn. I was looking forward to that part."

Tina laughed, her gaze tangling with his. He bent his head to kiss her temple, and she breathed his scent, basking in the warmth radiating from his body. Luke was as smart as he was attractive. She had to be on her toes. Between the sexual charge simmering between them and sidestepping his tricky questions, she felt more alive than she had for a long time.

In her life as Bettina Borlenghi, fashion industry maven, she couldn't ever be completely herself, the person she was deep down. Being in the public eye, holding her own in the business world, dealing with predators like Fabio, had forced her to build a hard shell. Consequently it took a lot to touch her heart. Fabio had been the last straw, the final injury that made her realize something in her life needed to change. But how did she get back to who she really was? Did she even know that person anymore?

Here in Luke's living room, she was starting to remember. Her blood fizzed with sparkling wine and his heated glances and she was just…Tina. This fling could be more than an opportunity for a sexual adventure. It was a chance to find out who she was again. To rediscover that sensual, free-spirited—*trusting*—woman she'd been before over-work, responsibility, and disappointment had sucked a lot of the joy from her life.

Luke clinked his glass with hers. "To honesty and trans-parency. There's so little of it in this world. It's refreshing to meet someone who is exactly what she seems."

"An odd toast." Tina sipped demurely, eyes averted. She

was walking a tightrope. On the one hand, she wanted Luke to know her, the *real* her. On the other, she was terrified to peel back the layers in case he disliked what he found. "So you think I am exactly what I seem. Tell me, what is that?"

"I was being tongue in cheek. I think you're a mass of contradictions." He clasped her fingers and brought them to his lips as he held her gaze. "You seem more like someone who *has* assistants than someone who *is* an assistant. You're too elegant, too independent, too assertive to be a sales assistant."

"Oh? How many sales assistants are you intimately acquainted with?" She smiled when he remained silent and withdrew her hand. It was a risky game but oddly fun. "None, obviously. I thought so. You found me working in the boutique. What else would I be but a salesclerk?"

Smiling slightly as he studied her, he seemed to be enjoying the challenge, too. "You're too curvy to be a model—"

Her chin came up on a spurt of defensive anger. "Are you saying I'm f—"

"I'm saying you're gorgeous. Soft. *Sexy*." Luke continued to regard her thoughtfully. "You could be a buyer…."

"What does it matter who I am?" She dropped her voice to a low purr. She needed to remind him—and herself—why they were here. Referencing her cowboy fantasy she tried to distract him. "Maybe I'm a dancing girl in a saloon, and you've come upstairs so we can get better acquainted."

"I certainly hope we will." He slipped an arm around her waist and nuzzled her neck, speaking in her ear. "But you're a puzzle. I've never met anyone like you."

Her eyelids drooped at his warm breath on her neck. Every inch of her was alive and burning beneath his touch.

"Don't try to solve me. Let's just enjoy each other."

"Trust me, our mutual pleasure is exactly what I'm aiming for." His eyes darkened as his gaze dropped to the curve of her breasts. "But I've dated waitresses and socialites and all sorts of women in between. I can tell the difference between cheap and expensive perfume. Yours is as expensive as they come."

"Duty free. An extravagance, I'm afraid." The banter, the smoldering looks, the sizzling touches. No, she definitely didn't want this fling to come to a crashing halt. She didn't want the ruse to end. Maybe by pretending to be someone else, she could actually find herself…

She slid her hand down his chest to his abdomen. He sucked in a breath. Rock hard pecs and sculpted abs, the body of an athlete. Lower still, she palmed the large bulge in his pants. "Let's cut to the chase." She worked the supple leather of his belt out of the gold buckle. "Is that the correct idiom? Cut to the chase?"

"Are we talking cowboys and outlaws, or me chasing you around the four poster?" He trailed kisses behind her ear, his breath warm on the sensitive skin of her neck, and ran his fingers across her bare midriff, making her stomach muscles ripple in response.

"Oh, the four poster, definitely." She undid his zipper and plunged her hand inside his boxers, curling her fingers around his thick erection. His shirt was completely open and his pants were a mere tug from coming down. She was burning up, dying to feel his body pressed against hers.

"Seems to me…" he murmured, tugging her top and bra down to expose her breast to his questing mouth. "The chase is over."

Tina's head fell back as she gave herself up to the sensation of his lips and tongue on her bare skin. His mouth and hands grazing her nipples. Heat spread through her. Jet lag dissipated as if by magic. The mild headache she'd fought, long forgotten. The anger, hurt, and resentment her dealings with Fabio and the public humiliation he'd subjected her to, even the good things—her family and her work and her friends in Rome—all fell away beneath Luke's touch.

She needed him. She wanted him so badly. A man who, even if he had suspicions she wasn't who she'd claimed to be, didn't care who she was or what she did for a living. A man who saw her as a woman, period. It was a heady fantasy, more potent than cowboys or pirates or any other costume, to think their fling could be something real and lasting. But that was impossible, too much to wish for. At best, she would have a few nights of pleasure. Warm memories to wrap around her when she returned to her real life.

Tina pulled off her top and tossed it away, along with her wistful yearnings. Then she unzipped, shimmied her hips, and her skirt slid to a puddle on the hardwood floor. Her strapless bra bunched beneath her breasts, the demi-cups that he'd shoved aside creating even more décolletage. The matching G-string in red satin accentuated the full curves of her hips.

Luke's eyes burned. Flashes of red rode on his high cheekbones as he stripped off his pants and shrugged out of his shirt. "Come here." His voice was as rough and bumpy as a road through the Wild West. Now he was more outlaw than good guy, dangerous and exciting with his intense blue gaze, his broad shoulders and, yes, his huge cock. "I want you."

With equal parts anticipation and apprehension, she

stepped into his embrace. His arms closed around her, and he started to lift her. Instead, she wriggled back to the floor. "Let me taste you." She pressed tiny kisses to his abdomen. Between each kiss she licked and then blew on his wet skin. "Do you like that, cowboy?"

"Don't know if I'm shivering or burning up," he said, his voice raw.

Tina ran cool fingers over the ridges and indentations in his abs, down the lines of his groin to his rock hard penis ridged with veins. The skin was like hot silk over steel. "You feel so good."

Then her mouth closed over him. With a shudder, Luke speared his fingers through the thick dark mass of her hair and dragged her up. "I said, come here."

Their tongues clashed and tangled in a frenzy of wet, open-mouthed kisses. His huge hands splayed across her body, touching as much of her as he could. She rubbed against him, trying to get closer still. He flicked the catch on her bra and tossed it away. Then he filled his palms with her breasts, his thumbs running across her nipples. Her eyes closed as he lowered his mouth to the rosy-brown peak of an erect nipple. He sucked and pulled and his cock dug into her belly. He shifted his leg until she was riding his thigh, pressing herself against his hard muscle, seeking ease from the throbbing, aching need between her legs.

He pulled on her butt to bring her closer. His palms ran roughly over her cheeks and his fingers brushed down her crack beneath the slender band of fabric on her G-string.

"Get rid of it," she panted and he gave a yank, the sound of tearing fabric mingled with their harsh breathing. He adjusted their positions, then his fingers penetrated her wet core while his tongue mimicked the thrusting motion.

"Oh, Luke. God." She took him in her hand again, stroking up and down his shaft, squeezing, wanting him inside her. She was breathing hard and every cell in her body pulsed with a bright energy.

"You're so fucking beautiful," Luke whispered, tracing the outside curve of her breast with the edge of his knuckle while his gaze devoured her. "I want to fuck you so hard."

Her knees turned liquid. "Do it, do me. Fuck me now."

He dropped to his knees, his hands sliding down the outside of her legs and back up her inner thighs, spreading her open for his mouth. Her legs trembled, and she braced her hands on his shoulders, palms curving around his muscles, flexing and contracting as he caressed and stroked her.

His tongue found her clitoris and the electric jolt almost lifted her off the ground. He circled and licked, flicking it with his tongue and sucking, driving her crazy. She sagged against him, head drooping as she struggled to hold back her orgasm.

"You taste so fine. Come for me, babe." He inserted two clever fingers and probed the most sensitive spot just as he pressed down on her clit with his hot, moist tongue.

"*Mio Dio. Tu sei caldo.*" Her long moan of pleasure erupted into a stream of Italian. She pumped her hips into his face—and came and came and came. While she was still limp, he caught her up in his arms as if she was no more than a rag doll and carried her through the living room to a bedroom.

He laid her on a king-sized bed, the silky coverlet cool beneath her heated skin. She caught a glimpse of stars, their subtle glow shining through the vaulted skylight, before

Luke loomed over her, his weight causing the bed to dip.

She reached up, clasping his biceps to pull him to her. "I want you inside me," she breathed. "Now."

. . .

"Yes, ma'am," Luke teased, making fun of her tendency to direct proceedings. "There's nowhere else I'd rather be." She'd soon find out who was in charge. Fact was, though, Luke wanted her so badly it was fucking primeval. Placing a splayed hand on Tina's belly where a pulse beat high and hard, he reached into the drawer in his bedside table for a condom.

Her eyes were dark and searching and her upper thighs glistened with traces of her own juices. He tore the plastic with his teeth. His cock was so hard it hurt, and he winced as he quickly sheathed himself. It took every ounce of his control to stop himself from plunging into her the moment he was protected.

But despite her demands, he was going to make sure she was ready for him again. And the second time would be even better than the first for her. He straddled her and lowered himself to his knees and elbows. Then he made it his business to coax those luscious soft nipples back to stiff peaks with his mouth and fingers. His erection throbbed against her stomach, but he held onto his control and lavished attention on her breasts. Amazing breasts. Full and firm above the ridges of her ribs.

But his little Italian wasn't so easily dissuaded. He groaned when she wrapped her slender hand around his cock and roughly guided him to her entrance. "I want you inside me." With a thrust of her hips, he was captured.

Gripped by her tight heat he became almost dizzy with lust. "You're a bossy little thing, aren't you?" he breathed against her forehead.

"I'm not exactly little." Eyes half-closed, she writhed beneath him, grinding her hips into his. "You're not either. You feel amazing."

"You're so tight. Tight…and hot…and sweet." Sweat popped on his forehead with the effort of keeping himself in check. Slowly he withdrew and thrust into her again with a long, slow stroke, torturing them both.

Tina groaned and thrashed, knocking pillows off the bed. Her nails scraped down his back. "Fuck me, cowboy. Ride me hard."

Sweeter words were never spoken.

"It will be my pleasure." Bracing his hands on the padded leather headboard, he thrust hard into her. She was smaller than him but she was strong, her muscles bracing to take the force and meeting him with hard thrusts of her hips, like a bucking bronco. They might have only teased at playing out some saloon style scene, but he friggin' loved the way she'd responded to him. No holding back. No games. All pleasure.

His body was slick with perspiration, creating a slapping sound when they came together in a rhythm that rocked the bed and made it thump against the wall.

Tina's lips were drawn back, her eyes wild, and her whole body taut and charged, as if she was driven to wring every last drop of desire and sensation out of herself—and him. She was sexy and insatiable, and she was hands-down the best fuck he'd had in a long time. No, make that *ever*. Definitely.

If he didn't slow the hell down, the best sex of his life would be over before he had a chance to fully savor his sweet, sexy Italian.

He changed the pace, adjusting his angle and catching his breath, taking a moment to suck on her peaked nipples. She was breathing hard, too, her smooth olive skin glistening. The musky scent of their fucking enveloped him like a tropical night. Tina's eyes closed as he ground his pelvis into hers. She moaned and bit her bottom lip as he hit her sweet spot. Snatches of Italian emerged between pants, and her ever-gesturing hands punctuated her words even in extremis.

Then her hips lifted in a prolonged thrust, and she clung to his shoulders. Luke pumped strongly and steadily. He knew the moment she came, her inner muscles clenching impossibly tight around him. Bliss washed the tension out of her face and limbs and she went limp in his arms. As she lay beneath him, suspended in ecstasy, he gave one, two, three final thrusts and shuddered out his own explosive climax.

Luke lowered himself carefully and rolled them both over, still inside her. Arms wrapped around her, his heart rate slowly returned to normal and his breathing slowed. Easing back a little, he blew on her damp forehead, ruffling tiny dark curls that stuck to her skin. "You okay? I didn't hurt you, did I?"

"*No, sto benissimo. Grazie mille.*" She held his jaw with her fingertips and effusively kissed along the angle and down his neck. "*Sei fantastico!* You make me glad I'm a woman."

"That makes two of us. Glad you're a woman, that is." A chuckle rumbled in his chest. "I'm more than happy to be the man."

She shifted, easing off him and snuggled in close, one

arm flung across his chest. He took a moment to dispose of the condom then tucked her back under his arm, more than content to doze until they recouped enough to start again. Maybe ten minutes or so....

• • •

Luke awoke slightly disoriented. The lights were still on in the living room but the bedroom was in darkness. Next to him, Tina was breathing evenly, eyes closed. She'd shifted position onto her back. Her arm was flung wide, exposing those sexy as hell breasts. The curve of her hips tapered to a neat thatch between her thighs. He wanted another taste. His body began to stir back to life.

Then he glanced at the clock. Five am. They'd slept a good four hours. He got up to use the bathroom. When he returned, Tina was also up, muttering to herself as she wriggled into her leather skirt.

"I have to go." She turned her back to him so he could zip up her skirt while she dragged on the red top. "*Per favore.*"

Instead, he slid his arms around her waist and planted kisses on the back of her neck. "Stay the night. We're not finished yet."

"I'm so sorry, *mi amore*, but I have an early meeting, remember? I wish I could stay but I can't." She kissed him and for a moment melted into his arms, warm and soft and compliant. "You've been wonderful, spoiling me with beautiful food and champagne, making amazing love to me. It was a perfect night." Then she pulled away reluctantly. "I have to go."

"Come back to bed," he coaxed. "I have to get up early,

too, to coach hockey. I'll set the alarm and then take you wherever you need to go in the morning."

"No." There was a strange quality to her voice and she averted her gaze. "I must leave now. Could you call me a taxi, please?"

"I'll drive you home." He found a pair of pants and dragged them on. "Where do you live?"

"I don't want to put you to any trouble," she insisted. "I'll take a cab."

"It's no trouble." He could be stubborn, too. "I don't let women grab a taxi off the street in the middle of the night when they leave my place."

"Then I will be the first." She slipped into her shoes, grabbed her purse and made her way through the apartment to the front door. Only to be confronted by his security system. "So many locks. *Madre mia*!"

He was tempted to keep arguing, but he didn't want to ruin the time they'd shared, so he compromised. "I'll come down to the street and wait with you." Luke unlocked the door and scrambled into his shoes. As they rode down in the elevator he pulled her into his arms and kissed her, entertaining a brief fantasy of sex in the elevator. Then a woman got on with her French bulldog out for an early morning walk, and he had to keep his hands to himself.

On the street, he paced the curb, scanning oncoming cars for a cab to flag down. Traffic was light and every taxi that passed was occupied. Tina scrolled through the messages on her phone. She seemed to have a lot.

"I'll call you tomorrow," he said. "I mean, later today."

"Oh!" Her fingertips went to her mouth as if she'd just thought of something. "When do you come in to work?"

"I'm normally there when the bar opens at ten thirty. But today I've got business to take care of in the morning. Probably won't get in until noon." He planned to call his old teammates to see if they'd be willing to help with fundraising. Thinking of that he smiled, recalling how Tina had offered to help. It was really nice of her considering she barely knew him and didn't know the kids at all. But he needed a lot more than she could afford. Speaking of which, he needed to get a hold of some of the newscasters on ESPN. He could try the local sports reporters. Maybe hit up players from the other sports teams in the city…

"Will you call me when you're done?" she asked, breaking into his thoughts.

"Of course." He spotted an oncoming taxi and flagged it down. He had time for one more quick embrace then Tina leaped in the car, blowing kisses and smiling.

"Wait. How far is your hotel?" He reached automatically for his pocket, but his wallet was upstairs in his loft. "Let me pay your fare."

"No. No." She made a shooing wave toward the driver, instructing him to go. "*Ciao, amore. A presto.*"

"*Ciao.*" The taxi pulled away and she was gone, leaving Luke a little dazed, standing with his hands in his pockets as dawn lightened the patches of sky between the skyscrapers. The abrupt end to what had been the best sex of his life was a bit surreal. In retrospect, the whole evening had an unreal air about it, as if it was too amazing to be true. As if Tina was too sexy and beautiful and fun to be real.

Her evasiveness was troubling, and the way she'd sped off before he could hear her address or even offer to pay, he didn't think that was an accident. His spidey senses went on alert whenever someone didn't answer questions directly. His mother had been a master at hiding her movements and covering what she was up to. He didn't ever want to deal with anyone like that again. Not that he thought Tina was a gambler, but she was hiding *something*.

His interest in her was purely sexual, of course. He didn't do relationships. He'd never seen one that worked. After the number Mom had done on him and his family, and the scores of girls and rink rats that chased him for his fame or former glory…nah, he wasn't into anything permanent.

Still, he was scratching his head as he went back inside his apartment building. She'd told him not to try to "solve" her but he was a curious guy. He wouldn't be able to help himself.

Chapter Five

Tina entered the radio station sound booth and beamed a smile at Rob and Amy, an attractive talk show duo in their late twenties. According to Charmaine, they were the highest rating morning drive time program in New York.

Rob and Amy chattered away, trading insults and jokes in a fast-paced patter. Charmaine sat in a corner behind Tina as backup in case she was asked a tricky question. No stranger to interviews and dealing with the media, Tina closed her eyes to mentally prepare herself. But having had only a few hours' sleep, she drifted off into a pleasant reverie about Luke, naked and powerful, inside her. The way he'd looked into her eyes, he made her feel so sexy... And when he kissed her, *Dio mio*, she'd thought she would combust on the spot. Tired as she was, warmth spread through her to all her aching intimate parts.

He was a giver, very different from Fabio. Fabio had taken not just her money and her sexual favors but also her heart and self-esteem, and he'd given almost nothing in return. He'd been fun, but not as good in bed as he liked to think. The fun paled when there was nothing substantial in his character. He was a talented photographer or she wouldn't have bankrolled his business. But how could she have defended him even when her brother Giorgio had unearthed evidence of Fabio's previous arrest for swindling a woman in France? Her only excuse was temporary insanity.

Luke, on the other hand, was not only generous and giving, he already had his own business, clearly a successful one. He was honest, too. Unlike her. She squirmed on her cushioned studio chair. How would he feel if he knew she'd lied to keep her true identity from him? She'd had several opportunities to tell him, and she'd shied away. He only had to pop into the boutique while she was there for the jig to be up. Luckily he wouldn't be around this morning while she was at the opening, and after today she wouldn't be spending much time at the boutique due to promotional events that required her presence.

Who she was didn't matter, she reasoned, if they were just having a fling. He knew she wasn't sticking around, that they could never be a couple. In less than a week, she would be gone from New York. No doubt she'd be back and forth at intervals to see how the boutique was doing, but her work, her family, her life—everything she held dear—was in Rome.

She'd hated having to leave in such a rush, practically in the middle of the night. If she hadn't, if he'd insisted on driving her home, things might have gotten dicey. *Dio*. What if he happened to be listening to this station during her interview? He would no doubt recognize her voice. Then she remembered his hockey practice and relaxed.

She checked her phone. No calls or messages. Her thumbnail found the tiny chip in her nail polish and scraped it a little bigger. Was he mad at her? Maybe thinking twice about having anything to do with that crazy Italian lady? She sent him a quick text. *Thanks for last night. I had a wonderful time.*

A flashing green light indicating the end of a commercial break brought her back to the studio and she tucked her phone away.

"We're chatting live to Bettina Borlenghi, head of high end fashion atelier, House of Borlenghi." Amy signaled to Tina, counting down seconds with her fingers. "Bettina, welcome to New York. I understand you're about to open a new boutique on Madison Avenue."

"*Sì, grazie*, Amy." Tina pushed Luke from her mind and sat up straighter. She was here to promote her fashion collection, not daydream about a man. "I'm *molto* excited about Borlenghi Boutique and especially my fall collection, seen for the first time anywhere right here in New York."

From the sidelines, Charmaine gave her a thumbs up.

Roy broke in, grinning to show he was joking around. "I'm a dude who knows nuthin' from nuthin' about fashion. Is it different in Italy compared to America? Do guys really wear those floppy velvet hats?"

"Only the gondoliers in Venice," Tina replied then smoothly segued back to her primary message. "Women everywhere in the world want to look their best and to feel special. They want clothing that is on trend but at the same time, unique. At Borlenghi Boutique, we specialize in one-off pieces that are timeless."

The interview went on for ten minutes of intelligent

questions from Amy and amusing interjections from Roy. Tina managed to mention the fashion show three times and the location of the boutique four times.

After it was over, Charmaine shepherded her through the building and onto the street where the white limo was waiting.

"That was fabulous," Charmaine said when they were heading uptown for the official opening ceremony of the boutique. "You seem tired though. Are you going to be okay? You don't need to stay long at the store. Just cut the ribbon and say a few words to the staff and any customers."

"I'm fine. Just jet-lagged." Tina touched up her lipstick in a pocket mirror. "Did you order the pastries and Prosecco?"

"I got almond biscotti instead," Charmaine said. "Is that okay? I didn't think it was a good idea to hand out sticky pastries to people who might be trying on clothes."

"*Perfetto*. You're brilliant."

The line of women waiting for the boutique to open stretched from the front doors to the end of the block and around the corner. The limo pulled up in front of a red carpet leading into the store. A doorman hired for the day was on hand. Reporters and photographers milled about on the sidewalk. As soon as the car stopped, flashbulbs began snapping.

"*Benissimo*!" Tina clapped her hands. "What a fabulous job you've done! You didn't tell me about all this."

"Well, there were so many things to think of." Charmaine waved away the praise. "Shall we?"

Tina emerged from the limo to applause and more flashing cameras. TV news reporters clamored for her attention backed by cameramen. She answered questions as she slowly made her way to the store. With this kind of promotion her boutique would be off to a flying start.

The windows of Hat Trick were still dark but it was only nine am and the bar didn't open till ten thirty. Thank goodness Luke wasn't here to see her grand entrance. By the time he arrived at noon, she would have left for her next appointment.

Turning away from the reporters, she stopped to chat to the women waiting in line, inviting them to have a sparkling wine with her when the doors opened in fifteen minutes. Charmaine gently dragged her away and ushered her inside to introduce her to Janelle, a chic brunette in her forties, and the sales assistants, Pam, Amanda, and Kylie, who were so slender and stylish they could have been models. All four women were wearing complimentary articles of clothing of their choice from her collection. They paused their last minute tasks of polishing counters, setting out the tray of biscotti and adjusting the display racks to greet her. Tina ignored proffered hands and kissed them all on both cheeks, saying a few words to each in turn. Pam, the youngest salesgirl, was so overcome, she curtsied. Tina laughed and squeezed her hand, bringing her upright.

"*Grazie mille* for making the opening of Borlenghi Boutique a success." Spreading her arms wide to encompass everyone, she added, "*Siete tutti belli*. You are all beautiful."

Then the doors opened. Customers flooded in. Tina handed out flutes of Prosecco and talked—to customers, to window-shoppers, to reporters. To an old man wearing rags who wandered in looking for free food. Charmaine tried to shoo him out. Tina led him to the refreshments and found him a chair, leaving him looking bewildered but pleased.

Sales racked up steadily on the electronic cash register. Excited, happy women exited the store with multiple shopping bags. By late morning, the initial frenzy had morphed into a steady stream of customers. Tina decided she had to take a break before she collapsed. "I'm going back to my hotel to get some rest," she said to Charmaine as she texted Frank to pick her up in the limo. "I only had a few hours of sleep last night."

"Jet lag's a bitch," Charmaine agreed. "This has been a great kick off to launch week."

"I'll be back later this afternoon for closing," Tina promised Janelle. She grabbed a broad brimmed hat to shield her face in case Luke was at the bar and slipped out the door, hurrying straight into the waiting limo. "St. Regis Hotel, please."

She checked her messages on the way and smiled with relief. Luke had texted back, asking when he could see her. Thank goodness her abrupt departure last night hadn't put him off. She hit the keypad to reply. *I'll call you this afternoon after the boutique closes. We'll do something fun.*

The car was stuck in traffic so she used her spare few minutes to do an Internet search and found images of him as a hockey player. *Bellissimo!* He looked like a sexy Viking when he sported a full reddish-blond beard. She clicked through more links—so many awards and achievements— and came upon information about his disabled children's sports foundation. *Dio*, he'd done so much for those kids. A press release dated only this morning spoke about the financial trouble it was in. Her eyes widened as she read on. Big trouble. Thoughtfully, she made note of his financial advisor's name. She would give Luke a token amount that a salesclerk could afford. Then she would go through this Allan Montes to make a substantial donation — anonymously.

. . .

"Hey, Rosie," Luke greeted his bartender as he strode through the bar around midday. Hockey practice had gone well. The kids were pumped about the upcoming game and maybe making the finals. He hadn't had the heart to burst their bubble so he didn't said anything about the possibility of losing funding. Anyway, that wasn't going to happen. He would find the money if it was the last thing he did.

Rosie, with scarlet pig-tails and full sleeve tatts on her arms, looked up from restocking the fridge behind the bar with bottled beer. "Hey, Luke. Did you see the crowds next door?"

"Crazy, huh?" He'd glanced through the boutique's windows hoping for a glimpse of Tina but it was hopeless given the hordes of women in there. It could be hours before she got a break.

As he passed the kitchen, he paused to watch Luis, the chef, prepping tapas for the lunch rush. "Luis, my man, is the new stove working okay?"

Luis, his dark hair tucked beneath a white cotton cap, looked up from a tray of chorizo and patatas bravas and grinned. "Fantastic, boss."

"Excellent." Luke went into his small office at the back of the bar and shut the door. He called his manager Roy and explained the situation, asking him to book a venue for an exhibition game as soon as possible. "All the guys are on board. Yep, both teams. The tickets are going to sell out in minutes." Or so he hoped. "Can you do me one other favor? Get me a spot on ESPN so I can broadcast to the nation how badly these kids need support."

"I'll get right onto it," Roy said. "Sure would be a shame to lose the foundation after all you've done to build it up."

"Thanks, pal." Luke hung up and leaned back in his desk chair, wondering how Allan was doing with the bank. Fundraising was all well and good, but if the bank wouldn't extend a line of credit long enough for the money to start rolling in, then the foundation could still go under.

When he was a kid, a local charity had helped him buy ice skates and a helmet so he could join a hockey team that played on an outdoor rink. If he hadn't been given a leg up he wouldn't have had the career he did, or be where he was today. Now that he'd achieved success he wanted to give back. He needed to pay it forward.

Restless, Luke went out to the bar. A table of rowdy Australian tourists were watching Aussie rules football in the corner, and a handful of regulars were dotted around the place. He walked outside to check if the circus was still going on next door.

It was. Reporters milled around outside the boutique, snapping photos of the celebrities arriving for the launch as they were discretely whisked from limos past the queue and up the red carpet. The line-up to get into the boutique still stretched down Madison Avenue all the way to the other corner. Briefly he thought about going over there but he knew Tina wouldn't have time to talk, and he didn't want to cause her trouble with her hard-nosed boss.

A harried Allan emerged from the crowd of jostling women and slipped past Luke into the bar, straightening his tie and smoothing down his ruffled hair. "Whew! I took my life in my hands back there."

"Never get between a woman and a sale," Luke agreed. "By contrast to what's out there, this is a bastion of masculinity. What can I get you?"

"Just coffee," Allan said, sliding onto a high stool. "I'm working."

"And I'm trying to stay awake." Between making love to Tina and afterward wondering why she'd run off like that, he hadn't gotten a lot of sleep. Luke poured two cups of Colombian medium roast and filled Allan in on his fundraising efforts. "What happened with the bank?"

"I met with the manager this morning and asked for a line of credit. He said he'd think about it. I'm expecting a phone call with his answer any time." Allan dumped sugar in his mug and stirred, eyeing Luke curiously. "You look different. What happened?"

"What do you mean, different? I'm just tired."

"Not that. You're keyed up. Like you used to look at the start of the hockey season, just before a big game. Excited, ready to go." Allan gave him a sidelong glance. "Is it that sales assistant?"

Luke pulled up a stool next to Allen and sipped his coffee. "I don't know what you're talking about."

"You liked her. I could tell."

"Yeah, I like her. So what?" He liked her a lot. And she was so hot she was flammable. Not that Allan was getting any details out of him. He blew out a sigh. It wasn't all rosy. "Have you ever gone out with a woman who won't tell you anything about herself? Won't even let you take her home?"

Allan lifted his cup to his mouth. "Most of my dates in

high school were like that."

"Yeah, well, I've never encountered this problem before." Luke cupped his mug in his hands, his mind back in his bedroom at midnight with Tina naked, riding him. The crazy thing was, she seemed to like him too. At least she liked having sex with him. She was playful and inventive and she'd made him come like a freight train.

"So, what are you going to do about her?" Allan asked.

What he wanted to do was fuck her brains out at every possible opportunity. Trouble was, he didn't know when he was going to see her again. "She's kind of elusive."

"For a guy who's used to being in control I can see how that would rankle."

"I want to know where I stand."

"Don't question," Allan suggested with a shrug. "Just enjoy."

"Yeah, I guess." One of the Aussies, a tanned and fit thirty-something dude who looked as if he spent most of his life on a beach, came up to the bar and ordered another round. Rosie started to pour pitchers of draft beer. Luke waited until she left to deliver them to add, "Thing is, I want more than sex from her."

Allan's eyebrows rose. "You do have it bad."

"Oh, I don't mean anything long term or serious, necessarily. She's not going to be in town long. I'm okay with a fling. A little harmless fun between two consenting adults. But I wouldn't mind a few biographical details to make me feel as if I knew her."

"What have you got on her?"

"Her first name is Tina. I don't know her last name." Luke ticked additional points off on his fingers. "She's a sales assistant next door at the boutique. She's from Rome, Italy. She's always talking with her hands—it's super cute. She has an amazing body, and she knows how to use it. Her brother is a fan of the Naples soccer team and collects memorabilia. She likes pastries. She's sweet. She was concerned about the kids' hockey team and wanted to donate to the foundation." He thought for a moment. "And she has suspiciously excellent taste in champagne, food, and art."

"All good stuff but you're right, it's not much to go on," Allan agreed. "Can't you just ask her about herself?"

"I've tried." They kept getting sidetracked which he wasn't complaining about, mind you. He moved to take a tray of empty glassware from Rosie. While Luke loaded them into the washer, Allan took a phone call.

"Hit me with it," he said when Allan hung up.

"The good news is, the bank granted my request to extend you a short-term loan." Allan paused. "The bad news is, it'll barely cover the operating expenses and the interest rate is going to break you. You've still got to come up with a big chunk of cash, ASAP."

"Crap." Luke grabbed a stool and leaned on the bar. He'd been hoping for a quick fix but now the full implications of the disaster started to sink in. Sports venues were booked and paid for far in advance. A central office employed a dozen full-time coordinators and four or five people in each city. A break of even a few weeks would disrupt hundreds of lives and take many months or longer to repair.

"There's an alternative," Allan said. "You could shut the foundation down. No one would blame you. I can oversee the divestment of the resources, write it off on your taxes, even get someone to try to find other sporting programs for your kids."

An easy out. That's what Allan was offering him. He wasn't tempted, not for a second. How would he ever face the kids when they turned to him, trusting and confused, and wanted to know why they weren't going to be able to play anymore? "Nope, not an option," he said firmly. "I'll sell my left kidney before I shut down."

Allan grunted and didn't press. Luke ordered them something to eat, and they both fielded phone calls and made arrangements amid courses of chili prawns, Spanish tortilla, and patatas bravas.

Two hours later, a text pinged into Luke's phone. He tapped the screen to open. He smiled when he saw Tina's message, a ray of sunshine in a suddenly gloomy day. *I'm at the boutique, and I'm finished for the day. Are you up for a little fun?*

He quickly tapped a reply. *You bet. What do you have in mind?*

A pause and then, *How do you feel about role playing?*

His pulse quickened. While they'd only dabbled with the whole saloon girl/cowgirl scene, he was game for something more. *Like I said, I'll be anyone you want me to be.*

A few seconds later… *Hmm, so many possibilities. Who will you be tonight?*

He remembered the smoldering look in her eye when she'd grabbed his tool belt that first day and smiled. *I'm the handyman, at your service.*

"What's that grin about?" Allan said. "You look like the cat that ate the canary."

"Tina. We arranged to get together. She's letting me know she's ready."

Allan slid off his stool. "That sounds like my cue to leave." He clapped a hand on Luke's shoulder. "Catch you later, dude."

"Sure. And thanks." After Allan left, Luke went into his office at the back of the pub to find his work gear he kept there for odd jobs. He couldn't wait to be with her again and the fantasy element made it all the more exciting. He strapped on his tool belt, his spirits high. God knew he need-ed a distraction in the worst way. If anyone could take his mind off his problems it was Tina.

. . .

In the deserted boutique, Tina searched the lingerie rack for the sexiest corset, panty and garter set she could find and carried them into the third of the three fitting rooms. With four solid hours of sleep this afternoon she felt rested, refreshed and raring to go.

Opening day had gone off like a bomb, the crowds un-diminished all day until finally they'd shut the doors. Tina made an appearance a half hour before closing, congratulat-ed everyone, kept them enthused and smiling during clean up and then sent all the staff home.

Before Charmaine left, she reminded Tina of her din-ner tonight with fashion magazine editors. That wasn't for another three hours. Plenty of time for a sexy interlude. She clutched the bra and panty set and did a little happy dance. Luke would be her handyman. So exciting. She'd never got-ten her first impression of him out of her mind. The low-slung jeans, the snug T shirt, the tool belt…

And the role-playing, it leveled the field. Allowed

them both to pretend to be someone else. Granted her the freedom to just *be*.

She changed into the lingerie and slipped her "costume" skirt and top back on—an embroidered drawstring blouse and a peasant-style skirt in a filmy material. Then she tapped another message to Luke into her phone. *The door is open. Come in and lock it behind you.*

A few seconds later, her phone pinged. *On my way, bossy lady.*

Tina paced the plush carpet in high heels, jittery with anticipation. The luxurious fitting room contained a love seat and was lined with mirrors, including a three-way in one corner. She fluffed her hair and checked there were no flecks of mascara on her cheeks and that her lipstick hadn't smeared. Then she tugged down her blouse to expose the plump curve of her breasts and the top of her ivory and pink satin balconette bra.

The chime above the door sounded. She paused, listening. All she could hear was her heart thumping. A second later her phone pinged.

I'm here. Where are you?

She bit back a giggle. *In the fitting room. I've got a job I'd like you to do.*

She held herself totally still, listening for his footsteps, but the carpet was so thick, again there was nothing but silence.

Until the quiet snick of the first fitting room door opening. "Tina?"

She put her hand over her mouth so she wouldn't let out a sound and typed a message. *Keep looking.*

Ping went her phone. *I will find you…*

She swore she could feel the charged air between them even though she couldn't see or hear him. The second fitting room door clicked open. Then shut.

Getting warmer…

Are you ready for me?

He was standing right outside her door now. Her stomach was a hive of bees, all buzzing around, until she could hardly breathe. She arranged herself on the love seat in a sexy pose with her skirt rucked up between her slightly spread legs, one hand touching herself between her thighs. She was already slick and wet thinking about Luke and what he was going to do to her, and with her.

I am so ready…

Good. I brought my tool belt.

Her gaze was riveted on the door as it slowly opened. Luke filled the doorframe, his broad shoulders almost touching the sides, his tangled dark blond hair brushing the top. His sleeveless tank showed off sculpted biceps and a broad chest. His jeans were soft denim molded to long, strong thighs and an awe-inspiring package. His leather tool belt was slung around slim hips like a holster on a western lawman.

But it was his eyes that drew and held her gaze. They burned with a blue heat that sent the temperature in the fitting room skyrocketing. Tina licked her lips.

Luke took one look at her and quickly fell into her game. "I'm the handyman. What can I do for you?"

"I have a little problem," she said. "Between my legs. Can you handle that sort of thing?"

"I'll see what I can do." He entered the fitting room and suddenly the spacious area seemed cramped. His boot tread made imprints on the soft carpet, and his shoulder brushed the three-way mirror, making it swing forward. Now she could see herself, wantonly splayed, and Luke's back as he kneeled between her legs.

He gripped her thighs with both hands and gently pushed them farther apart. His thumbs slowly circled the sensitive skin on her inner leg. "Everything looks fine from here."

"It's farther up. Under the skirt." Tina's hold on the settee tightened as he slid the gauzy fabric up her leg, exposing the ivory silk of her panties. A gush of moisture flooded her. Her breath came shallower. "Can you see it now?"

One curled knuckle skimmed over her panties, down and then up, making her tingle. And again, adding a touch more pressure with each successive stroke until she was pulsing with need. He lifted his gaze to hers. Perspiration had formed on his upper lip. "Your 'problem' is behind this silk barrier. I'll have to remove it before I can go further. That okay with you?"

Tina, watching in the mirror, could see his broad, tapering back, one strong leg bent at ninety degrees. With his hands, big and tanned on her pale skin, so close to her core she had to fight for breath. "Do what you need to do."

"Hold still now. I don't want you to move an inch. It's a delicate operation."

She didn't want delicate. She wanted rough. She wanted his hands gripping her while he plunged that big tool of his where it would do the most good. Her whole body was screaming to move against his. "But—"

"No buts. I'm the professional. I say what goes."

Luke slid his hands up the backs of her thighs, lifting her

off the settee. With his fingertips he grasped the waistline of her panties and tugged slowly. He got them off almost to the point where her neat thatch of dark hair would be revealed and stopped.

"What's the matter?" she asked, panting. When she shifted her legs now she could feel the slippery slide of her juices against her swollen lips. The pulse had become insistent, demanding. "Why have you stopped?"

"To do a job properly the whole area has to be inspected." Heat darkened his blue eyes as he grasped the drawstring of her blouse and released the bow. The neckline sagged open, and he tugged it further down, exposing the curve of one breast and an enticing rim of pink lace. "It's an OHS issue."

"Occupational Health and Safety?" Her gaze dropped to his fingertips moving over her breast, leaving a burning trail of sensitized flesh in their wake.

"Other Hot Spots. They can flare up."

"Is that a bad thing?" she said faintly. "It doesn't feel like a bad thing."

"It's a good thing. I need to make sure they're at maximum." He pushed her blouse down over her shoulder, exposing a plump, satin-covered breast. "Ah, now that's what I like to see."

Tina looked down. Her nipple was hard and peaked beneath the ivory satin, and her flesh quivered with every shallow, needy breath. She ached for him to take her into his mouth. She positively squirmed with desire. "P-please."

His gaze shot to hers, full of heat and humor and his own controlled desire. "Remember what I said. Don't move. Trust me. I know what I'm doing."

Trust him? She didn't trust any man. But she did believe Luke knew what he was doing when he pulled her bra down and closed his hot mouth over her aching nipple. Oh, sweet torment. Every tug, every wash of his abrading tongue, every caress of her breast with his callused fingers sent her further into meltdown. Her limbs softened, and she sank deeper into the soft cushions, letting him do whatever he liked to her. She glanced at herself in the mirror. He'd unhooked her bra and both breasts were exposed, the round, heavy mounds cupped in his kneading hands while he kissed his way down her naked belly. Her panties were still half on, half off.

"Don't forget...the...job I wanted you to do," she said. "There's flooding. And it feels like...*il fuoco*. Fire. *Il fuoco della passione*. Ohhh" She lifted her hips, desperately trying to get closer to his mouth, his tongue, his hands, anything to relieve the pressure building in her.

"Almost there." Lust thickened his voice. "We need to finish preparing the site."

"It's fine. All ready to go. *More* than ready."

"I'll be the judge of that." He pulled her panties down another inch. A waft of cool air hit her moist folds, followed by a gust of warmth as Luke breathed out, his gaze fixed on her. "You are one pretty lady. Just a bit more prep...need to open you properly." He lowered his mouth to her and his tongue found the sensitive nub of her clitoris. A light brush before he circled her hips with his arms, pinning her arms down and holding her to him while he explored the flower-like folds, sucking and licking.

She wanted to touch him, too, but she couldn't move. It was torture at the absolute max. Thrashing her head to one side she clamped her teeth onto her blouse and pulled so hard in frustration that it ripped.

Perspiration had beaded on his forehead when he raised his head and her juices glistened around his mouth. He kissed her lips then, and she could taste herself, taste the sweat on his skin, breathe the pheromones swarming thick as a cloud around them. He drew back and pulled his shirt off over his head. More shining skin and sculpted muscles.

"Don't move," he ordered and started to unbuckle his tool belt.

"Leave it on. *Per favore.*" She reached out and drew a finger down his belly, following the thin arrow of hair to where it disappeared below the wide, supple leather.

"I told you not to move." He unhooked a roll of black electrician's tape and grabbed her wrists, winding the tape several times around them swiftly, before she had time to say or do anything. "This is a job for a master tradesman."

The mirror reflected a woman Tina barely recognized, on the brink of sexual disintegration. Her hair was wild, a curling dark brown mane that flowed over bare breasts and belly. Strips of clothing remained, torn and tangled. Her lips were red and swollen, mirroring the lips between her thighs. Luke skimmed off his pants, leaving the tool belt on. In the reflecting glass, she watched his butt muscles flex as he stepped out of his jeans. Thighs and calves strongly muscled from all that ice skating. She dragged her gaze away to the front of him.

His erect cock jutted toward her, long and thick and richly veined, emerging from a nest of dark golden curls. The strain of maintaining control was starting to show in the taut lines around his eyes and mouth, and the tight flex of his biceps as he tore open a condom. She would have taken him in her mouth, but he stood just out of reach, and he'd told her not to move. Anyway, she couldn't concentrate. All she could think of was getting him inside her.

"It's time to go in and finish the job." He adjusted her hips and she let him, limp and compliant. Every cell in her body pulsed in concert with the insistent throb between her legs. Then he picked up her hips and brought her to him, the head nudging at her entrance.

Tina closed her eyes and gave herself over to simply feeling. The stretch, the push, the incredible urgent need to engulf him, to take him inside and have him fill her. Then her eyes opened. She wanted to see his shaft disappear inch by inch into her, see the heat in his eyes when they melded, see the bunch and flex of his muscles as he strained to hold her and control their movements. For someone used to talking with her hands, without them she was mute. She pleaded with him with her eyes.

"I'm going to go in hard, okay? It's the only way to fix this...problem of yours."

Tina nodded eagerly. Hard. Yes. That's exactly what she wanted.

He crouched over her, one hand holding her butt, the other braced against the wall behind her head. He found her entrance, positioned his cock, then drove it home like a hammer blow. Again and again. Long, strong, hard thrusts that jolted her spine and touched a match to the powder keg of desire that was ready to explode inside her. Kaboom. Suddenly she was wild. She hooked her locked hands behind his head and pulled him down to her, ravaging his mouth the way he was ravaging her body.

He fell on top of her and together they rolled onto

the floor, bucking and slamming into each other. A pair of pliers fell out of his tool belt and dug into the back of her thigh. She rolled over, straddling him, her hands still taped and looped behind his neck. Her breasts pressed against his chest, and she ground her hips into his, feeling the cold brass buckle of his tool belt on her belly with every thrust. All the distractions faded into nothingness, and she gazed into his eyes. Intense. Heated. Blue. So blue. Blue like the Mediterranean. Like the silk thread on the blouse hanging around her neck. Blue like the skirt up around her hips.

Heat and hardness. Blond and blue. Luke filled her vision. Filled her inside. Enclosed her in his arms. Pounding, thrusting. Nothing soft or deferential. Nothing deceitful. He was what he seemed. A man who liked to fuck. Who liked to fuck her. Harder. Harder. Harder. Harder…

She heard his guttural groan at the same time she cracked wide open. Arms high and legs splayed apart, she sank onto him, into his bones and skin, soft and pliable as warm beeswax. She could feel the frantic beat of his heart. Hear the rasp of his breath next to her ear. Feel the pulse of his groin against her belly…

After what seemed like a long time, her brain came back slowly, lazily. In no hurry, even though she was lying on a fitting room floor in her empty boutique doing things she never thought she would do with a man she barely knew.

Had she ever had sex this good? Never. What was it about Luke? Tying her hands! She'd never done anything like that before. The electricians tape was biting into her wrists, hurting. She didn't care. The pain reminded her she was with a real man. A man who wanted nothing from her except the pleasure they could give each other.

To other women it might not be a lot to ask, but to her it meant everything.

Luke moaned, a satisfied sound that signified contentment down to his toes. His eyes fluttered open and he smiled at her. "Well, did that fix the problem?"

She wriggled her hips, savoring a blissful aftershock. "*Sì. Tu sei incredibile.*"

Chapter Six

Luke lay flat on his back on the plush carpet of the fitting room floor, completely shell-shocked. Fuck, that was good. Tina lay limp and boneless on top of him, wrapped in his arms. Her heart thundered against his, and her hair spread like a curtain across her back and down his sides. In a corner of the room, her phone started to ping. She stirred, seemed to consider getting it, then collapsed onto his chest again.

Hell, her wrists were still bound. Carefully he sat up, bringing her with him, and brought her arms down between them. With a pair of wire cutters from his tool belt he snipped the tape off her wrists. "I hope that didn't hurt."

"I didn't feel a thing." She rubbed the faint red marks.

"Sure? You went awfully quiet after I tied you up."

"Of course I went quiet. Italians talk with these." She waggled her fingers in his face. "If we can't move our hands, our mouths don't operate properly."

A smile curled his lips. "I'll have to remember that."

"Are you saying I talk too much?" Playfully, she pushed his chest, making him rock backward.

He grabbed her around the waist to haul her down for another scorching kiss. Then he released her, tucking her waterfall of hair behind her ears. "No, I love the way you use your whole body to communicate. Seeing you in the mirror was awesome. In fact, let's try for a better angle." He lifted her hips and adjusted her so her butt was reflected in the mirror. His cock immediately sprang to life. He wished he was a contortionist so he could look at this view of her and fuck her at the same time.

On all fours she hovered above him, kissing him with hot, open-mouthed kisses. She dragged her breasts over his chest and brushed her pussy over the head of his erection but kept herself tantalizingly out of reach. She was salty and sweet, warm and soft and voluptuous, fragrant with sex and perfume and her own unique scent.

"I can't get enough you. I love how you taste and smell and feel," he growled. "I want to eat you up."

"You taste good, too." She licked his flat nipple and then bit down, hard enough to trigger a jolt of electricity straight to his cock. "Mmm, Luke, I love the way you are so hard again already. I want you. I want you inside me, fucking me. I want—" She broke off as her phone started up again. "*Madre mia*. It's work."

"You really need to set boundaries with that boss of yours." Luke pulled her down on top of him, aching with need but the ringing wouldn't relent. He groaned. "Are you going to answer that?"

"I should." She rolled off him and reached for the phone. "Yes?"

Luke watched her face transform from lush softness to an alert intelligence. Almost absently she reached a blind hand out for her bra. With a spurt of annoyance he realized she was already detaching from him and moving on to her next thing.

"I'll be there. *Ciao*." She hung up and threw him an apologetic glance. "I'm sorry. I didn't realize it was so late. I have to go."

"Go?" Luke repeated. She was really doing it, blowing him off again. "I thought we could grab a bite to eat and then head back to my apartment."

"I should have told you before, but I have a dinner appointment." She dragged on her blouse and turned to the mirror to straighten her hair.

A dinner appointment? What did that mean exactly? "Do you mean a date?"

"No, it's work, to do with the fashion show coming up in a few days. I…we are meeting with the editors of some of the big fashion magazines."

Was it his imagination or did she keep stumbling over her explanations of what she was doing in New York? This wasn't the first time. He caught her hand, keeping her with him. "Your boss works you too hard. Early start, late finish. When do you get time off?"

"This is launch week for the boutique. It's a busy time. I knew I'd be working long hours before I came." She ran a fingertip lightly across his lower lip. "I just didn't know I'd meet such a hot man next door." She said something in Italian that sounded positively molten and kissed him again. "Believe me, I'd much rather spend the evening with you."

He wanted to believe her. Maybe he was a fool but she

seemed sincere. After all, it was only a fling. Only about the sex. "All right."

Luke retrieved the missing tools that had fallen and tucked them back into his belt. From now on, whenever he wore this he was going to remember this encounter in vivid detail. It would be a good memory to have when she was gone. With that sobering thought, he finished dressing and then followed her out through the display racks of high end fashion.

Outside Tina locked up and dropped the thick ring of keys into a leather tote. Luke offered her a lift home. Once again, she insisted on catching a taxi. Why was he not surprised?

"It's no trouble," he said. "I'll wait while you get ready and then drop you at the restaurant." He simply did not believe she was going to dinner with important fashion editors looking like she'd just tumbled out of bed. The musk of their lovemaking clung to her and while that was a major turn on for him, he doubted her boss would be impressed.

"No, but thank you." She stepped into the street and, putting her fingers to her mouth, let out a piercing whistle. Brightening, she turned back to him. "When I was a girl and watched movies set in New York I thought whistling for a taxi was the most wonderful thing. I've always wanted to do it myself."

"Well, you're good at it." He pressed a finger to his ringing eardrum. "Why are you so secretive? Why are you running away? Don't you trust me?"

A taxi cut across two lanes and pulled up to the curb. Tina opened the door. "Of course I trust you." But she didn't sound at all certain.

Luke held onto the door and blocked her way so she couldn't get in. "Prove it. Tell me where you're staying."

With an exasperated flourish of her free hand, she said, "In a furnished suite."

He mimicked her gesture, frustrated as hell himself. "Uptown, downtown—?"

"Midtown. Why do you need to know this? You said who I am doesn't make a difference to how you feel about me."

"It doesn't but…" Did she live in a slum? Surely not. An expensive boutique who brought an employee over from Italy would put her up in decent accommodations. "We don't exist in a vacuum either. When you're not around, sometimes I feel as if you're not real. I don't know anything about you. What's your last name?"

Instead of replying she gave him a warm, lingering kiss that made his head spin. "*That's* really all you need to know. That I want you. And you want me."

"So this is just a fling," he said flatly. "Two strangers getting together for sex." And what was wrong with that? He'd done it plenty of times before. It's what *he* had wanted. Yet with Tina the thought left him strangely dissatisfied.

"Don't make it sound sleazy. You're not a stranger. I like you. More than I expected. So very much more." She caressed his jaw, running a thumb over his light stubble. "You look good in a beard. I looked you up on the Internet."

She could do a search on him, but he couldn't do the same to her. It wasn't right. He captured her fingers. "I like you too. That's why I want to know more about you."

"Then we lose some of the mystery, no? We don't need to prove anything to each other." It almost sounded as if she was pleading with him. While he was still thinking of a reply she ducked into the taxi and then stuck her head out of the window. "*Ciao, amore.*"

The cab entered the stream of traffic heading south to midtown. Why wouldn't she tell him where she was staying?

A horrible thought struck him. Was she *married*? He was a pretty tolerant guy. He had one taboo and one taboo only—married women. He couldn't believe Tina would lie about that. But now it all made sense with a sickening logic. If she was married that would account for her sudden disappearances, for not wanting to stay overnight, not telling him where she was staying. Not even telling him her last name so he couldn't track her down.

Fuck. Luke kicked a newspaper box hard enough to make the glass rattle. A well-dressed matron walking her Pekinese gave him a disapproving look.

Another taxi stopped a few feet away and let off a passenger. Luke lunged for the open door, got in and slammed the door. He tossed a fifty dollar bill at the driver. "Follow that cab up ahead, the one with the Greenpeace bumper sticker. I'll give you another hundred if you don't lose it."

The taxi set off at a low speed chase, crawling through rush hour traffic. Luke leaned on the back of the front seat, gaze fixed on the distinctive bumper sticker logo. A furnished studio in a walkup or a three star hotel was the kind of accommodation someone on a sales assistant's wages could afford. They passed the turnoff to his street. What were the odds that she was staying in his neighborhood?

Up ahead, Tina's taxi stopped. He felt like a stalker but he needed more information about her, even if just seeing her hotel wouldn't tell him if she was married or not. He did *not* cheat, would *never* break up a family. If she was married then no way would he continue with the fun and games.

"Pull over half a block ahead and wait," Luke said to his driver.

His taxi swerved and double parked outside a cafe. Amid the honking and shouting that ensued, Luke watched through the rear view window as Tina's cab pulled up in front of the St. Regis Hotel. Then his eyebrows shot up as the uniformed doorman opened the cab door and ushered Tina out, bowing and touching his cap. She gave him one of her brilliant smiles and palmed him a tip. Then she hurried up the red carpet and into the lobby of one of the fanciest hotels in New York.

What the hell? How could she afford to stay there? Had she been bullshitting him about what she did? Did she have a higher job description than mere sales assistant? What kind of company sent a clerk overseas to work, anyway? Man, he was all kinds of confused. Emotions from his childhood flooded back, associated with the first time he found his mom coming out of a bar after telling him she was visiting her sister. That night they'd had no dinner, and she'd insisted someone had stolen her wallet. He'd believed her—until he'd seen her wallet sticking out of her purse.

"Hey, buddy! I can't sit here all day," the cab driver yelled over the din of honking horns. "Whadya want I should do now?"

Luke found a couple of fifties and passed them over. "I'll walk from here."

He stood on the opposite side of the road and stared at the hotel. Should he go in and confront Tina? How? He couldn't ask for her at the desk. He didn't know her last name. He could just picture that conversation. You know,

Tina—short, sexy, Italian, lots of wavy dark hair? Sure she was memorable, but desk clerks dealt with hundreds of guests every day. And when it came to the privacy of protecting a hotel guest, he highly doubted they'd just hand over her room information.

Hang on a second…she might not even be staying there. This might be where she was having dinner with her fashion editors and her boss. It was possible her boss was staying there. It didn't answer the question of whether she was married or not. But now that he'd calmed down, he didn't think so.

He needed to think so he set off north again to walk the ten blocks to his apartment. She must really be worried about being late if she couldn't go home to change. She probably sat in the background and took notes while those haughty bitches pushed food around their plates and made insincere noises about how fabulous one another was. He hoped they weren't mean to her.

Halfway home he turned into a diner on a side street and sat in a booth at the window. Inside the plastic-coated menu a paper clipped note listed the daily special. Lasagna. Perfect. He was quickly coming to crave all things Italian.

The waitress came and he gave his order, then he got out his phone. There was a message from Allan asking how the fundraising efforts were coming and one from Roy letting him know he had a spot on Mike & Mike in two days' time.

Yet another text from his mother begging him to call her. Telling him she'd been going to Gamblers Anonymous and was clean. Yeah, right. The family had heard that one before, numerous times. Luke hesitated with his finger over the delete button. What if she was telling the truth this time?

He left it for now and moved on. Timmy had left a voice mail reminding him about their game the day after tomorrow, the last one before the playoffs. As if he'd forget. They needed to win to go into the quarterfinals.

He punched the button to return Timmy's call. "Hey, squirt. How are you doing?"

"I'm fine," Timmy said in his usual chirpy voice. "Did you get my message?"

"Yep. Don't worry, I wouldn't forget. We're going to blast the other team out of the water."

"My mom bought me a new hockey stick. I'm taping the handle right now."

"Awesome. You'd better sharpen the wheels on your chair, too, so you can zoom past the other forward on your way to shoot a goal."

Timmy giggled. "You can't sharpen wheels. They'd pop."

"Really? Oh, no, so that's what went wrong with the last team I coached." He slapped his forehead. "Don't tell anyone, okay?"

"I won't. If you promise not to tell anyone about my…" Timmy's laughter faded.

The sudden silence was awkward. Luke winced, pretty sure Timmy hadn't meant to bring up his secret. Only Luke and Stella knew that he had to wear diapers when he played because his spinal injury meant he didn't have control over his bladder and sometimes he couldn't get off the ice, into the bathroom and out of his protective clothing in time when he had to piss. The stark reminder of Timmy's disability only served to reinforce Luke's determination to keep the foundation going.

"Hey, don't sweat it," he said lightly. "Just be ready to

rumble."

"Okay, Uncle Luke. See ya."

"Bye, Ace." Luke hung up and reached for the icy lager the waitress had brought a moment ago.

His thoughts drifted back to Tina. While not everything about her added up, did he want to mess up the most intense fling of his life on the basis of vague suspicions?

No, he didn't know her last name or where she lived but did that matter? He knew the taste and scent of her, the soft silk of her skin. He knew how passionate and inventive she was in the bedroom—or fitting room. How quickly she learned what turned him on. How she purely enjoyed the physical act of making love. The way she looked deep into his eyes when she came slayed him. Apart from sex, he knew she was playful, empathetic and generous. Hardworking and smart and family-oriented. In many ways, he did know everything important about her. So what was the problem?

The problem was, how much "mystery" was he willing to accept? She'd admitted to "champagne tastes" so maybe this innocent act was all a ruse. His mother had been a bullshit artist and a consummate actress. She'd left him with a legacy of distrust. Maybe too distrustful. Tina was a stranger in town, and she didn't really know him. She could simply be protecting her privacy and that was smart.

Now he had to be smart and not fall for her. He had to remember this was a fling and not be seduced by hope that this time the future would somehow turn out differently than expected based on experience. He could do that. Hell, he'd been doing it his whole life.

Speaking of… He went back to his phone messages and found the one from his mom. His finger hovered over the button. Smart, remember? He hit delete.

. . .

In her hotel suite bathroom, Tina stripped off her clothes and gratefully stepped into a steaming shower. She was a little tender in intimate places but wonderfully invigorated. Her soapy hands retraced Luke's caresses, and she smiled to herself. In a very long and tiring day, he'd been the brightest moment. He was so masterful and knew exactly how to please her. For a glorious hour or so she'd forgotten...everything. She'd been just a woman, very thoroughly satisfied by her man.

Then her smile faded. Luke had been angry and suspicious when they parted. He didn't deserve to be lied to. God knew, she wanted to tell him the truth. How wonderful would it be to be completely honest and to know with certainty that he wanted her for herself and not for what she could do for him?

Normal people exchanged personal details as a matter of course. She should tell him everything, she really should. He'd said he didn't care who she was or what she did. Maybe she could trust him. Maybe he really did only want her for who she was inside. The thought made her tear up. It's what she dreamed of.

With a sigh she snapped off the tap and stepped out of the shower. She wasn't so stupid as to actually believe in the fantasy. With only a week in New York, this could never be anything more.

Hurriedly she dressed and did her hair and makeup. Downstairs Frank held the door for her at the waiting limo.

She settled into the leather seat and closed her eyes. What seemed like a split second later, Frank was opening her door. "We're here, ma'am."

She blinked, slightly disoriented. "*Grazie*, Frank. And it's Tina."

"Yes, ma'am." He ushered her from the car.

Tina. Couldn't she just be Tina? "I'll be about three hours. I'll text you when I'm ready."

Up the steps she went and into the dim, swanky interior of the upmarket Italian restaurant Charmaine had recommended. The maitre d' led her to the table where her chair was the last one vacant. Four of the Big Apple's top fashion magazine editors and Charmaine were already seated. Groomed and well-dressed, they looked up expectantly.

"*Ciao, tutti!*" And she was on. Greeting everyone by name, speaking to the waiter in Italian, feeding her neighbors from her own plate when she tasted a particularly good morsel, making sure she had a few words with every person at the table, asking about themselves so it wasn't just about business. Of course she also talked up the boutique and the theme of her latest collection and promised front row seats at the fashion show.

She was in her element here. This was her boardroom. These women were her colleagues—smart, savvy and ambitious. She liked them, and she liked the parry and thrust of making alliances, cutting deals, forging new markets.

Yet it wasn't all of who she was or even the most important part. Luke knew a completely different side to her. A loving, passionate side that had atrophied through fear. The dinner was a huge success, but she wished that at the end of it she could curl up in his arms and just be his woman.

It was nearly midnight when Frank came to pick her up. She sank into the limo's back seat and watched the bright lights of the sleepless city flit past. She hoped she hadn't blown it with Luke by being so evasive. Likely it was just a matter of time before he found out on his own who she was, or someone told him. If she worried that he was mad now, it would be nothing compared to how he would feel when he learned she'd deliberately deceived him. It was no use telling herself she didn't care what he thought about her, that she wasn't staying in New York long, that soon she'd be back in Rome. For her at least, their liaison was no longer just about the sex. She was falling for him. Maybe tomorrow she would tell him the truth. *Che sera sera.*

Back in her hotel suite she turned on her laptop to Skype her brother. Giorgio answered her video call on the first ring, his dark hair and classic Roman features filling her screen. "*Ciao. Come stai*?" She covered a yawn with her hand. "What's up?

"Fabio." Giorgio's dark brows pulled together in a frown. "He's up to his old tricks."

"I know about the blond Englishwoman. She doesn't bother me. I feel sorry for her. Do you think I should warn her or will that look like jealousy?"

"I didn't call about her," Giorgio said. "Fabio is suing you for breach of promise, claiming you promised to marry him and then went back on your word."

Tina gave an incredulous laugh. "After he defrauded me of several million euros! It will never stand up in court."

"I know that. He's being vindictive, trying to harass you. But it's going to cause a headache just the same." Giorgio paused then added grimly, "There's more. He's in Manhattan.

I've had him followed. He may try to see you so be careful."

"I was afraid he'd come here for fashion week. *Per tutti i santi*, will I never be free of that man?"

When she'd met Fabio in Monte Carlo she'd quickly become infatuated with the handsome blond northern Italian. At first he'd been wonderful, treating her with respect but not overly deferential. Something she'd appreciated at the time. Gradually his attitude changed, alternating between obsequious and demanding. She'd told herself that she was being silly, that Fabio loved her as much as she loved him. She proved her affection by buying him his own photography business. But it had taken her brother Giorgio to see through Fabio for what he really was, a conman who was taking her for whatever he could get. Such a man cared for no one but himself.

"I have our lawyers working on it. I wanted to tell you about the lawsuit myself before you read about it in the newspaper." Giorgio paused. "You look tired. How is everything going there?"

"The launch is proceeding smoothly, but the days are very long. I'm still jet-lagged." She rubbed her gritty eyes. "Can I ask you a favor? Could you authorize the sale of some of my shares in Borlenghi Holdings? I want to transfer a million American dollars to my New York account."

Giorgio's frown returned. "Does the boutique need financial help already?"

"No, it's a donation to a disabled children's sports foundation." Her brother's eyebrows rose, and she held up a finger. "Yes, it's a large amount but the charity is worthy."

"*Va bene*, I'm sure you know what you're doing. It'll take a few days to go through, though," Giorgio said. "Oh, Layla and I will be in New York on business for a few days later this week."

Layla's curling red hair and bright smile entered the frame as she draped her arms around Giorgio's neck from behind. "We're coming to your fashion show!"

"I'm so glad. It'll be wonderful to see some familiar friendly faces there." Tina felt a special connection to her sister-in-law. She'd hired the American lingerie designer against Giorgio's company policy because Layla was so talented and they'd become fast friends.

"Normally fashion shows are on during the day," she went on. "I want to make a splash, do something different, so I'm having mine at night. Afterward there'll be a cocktail party. Make sure you bring a ballgown. Giorgio will need a tux."

Her brother made a resigned sound, and Tina turned back to him. "Giorgio, could you do me another favor?"

He smiled indulgently. "Anything, *cara*."

"Remember that painting I bought last year when I was here scouting out locations for the boutique? The one of the girl in a forest. It's hanging over my dining table at the villa. Can you bring it to me? I want to make a present of it to someone."

"I'll bring it," Angela said. Tina's sister appeared at the edge of the screen, her head angled sideways and her messy blond hair falling over her eyes. "I'm coming to New York, too. Who's the painting for? A man? Have you fallen in love again?"

"She's only asking because *she's* in love," Giorgio teased.

"I am not." Angela swatted her brother on the shoulder. "Rico is a horrible man who's making my life miserable. I hate him."

Tina smiled affectionately at her siblings' squabble. She missed them so much. "No, nothing like that. It's a…parting gift." Something for Luke to remember her by when her time in New York was over and their bedroom frolics were a fading memory. To avoid further probing on their part she turned the questioning back onto Angela. "So who is Rico?"

"Rico Mancini is a top chef who owns three of the biggest restaurants in Florence." Angela sighed. "If I could win the account to supply his restaurants I could grow my business by ten percent, and maybe then Giorgio would be satisfied I'm fully capable of running Borlenghi Fine Foods."

"I handed autonomy to each of you for your own divisions," Giorgo protested. "What more do you want?"

Angela leveled him a look that spoke volumes about what was missing. R.E.S.P.E.C.T. Tina understood and sympathized. Angela was the baby in the family, and they all adored her—no one more so than Giorgio—but maybe because of that he thought she was too soft-hearted for a business career. He'd given her the opportunity though, and she was doing her best to pull it off.

"If *Signor* Mancini isn't buying your products he must be crazy," Tina said. "You source the best cheeses and salamis in Italy."

"And olive oils, balsamic vinegars, and dozens of other gourmet foods," Angela fumed. "Rico's not crazy. He just doesn't know yet how determined I am."

"I pity poor Rico," Layla said. "But he's a match for Angela in the stubborn stakes."

"This clash should prove interesting," Tina agreed, grinning. "Before I forget, are we having our annual family holiday on the yacht?"

Francesca, her other sister, poked her dark head in. The four of them laughed as they jostled for space. "We're discussing it right now. You'll be back for it, won't you? It's coming up quickly, in ten days."

Only ten days. Suddenly her time in New York seemed very short. "I wouldn't miss it, I can't wait to see you all."

"*Allora*," Giorgio said. "We'll let you go. See you soon. *Buonanotte.*"

"*Ciao ciao. Tantassimi baci a tutti.*" Kisses to everyone. She blew them the endearments and clicked off.

Sleep eluded her even though she was so tired. A lawsuit! Her only crime had been to be too generous. Too foolish. Suddenly she was filled with fresh doubt about revealing her identity to Luke. All her wistful yearnings for a man who wanted her only for who she was inside seemed naïve. Even good men, strong men, weren't always immune to the temptations and problems of being with a wealthy partner. Luke was facing financial difficulties. He seemed honest and hard-working, a man with integrity. But she'd believed in Fabio, too, at first. And she'd only known Luke a few days. Trusting Fabio had gotten her into deep trouble, trouble that wouldn't go away.

She wouldn't tell Luke who she was. Not yet. With Fabio in the same city, she felt very vulnerable. It would be nice to know that Luke was in her corner. And her time with him was increasingly important to her. She could feel herself opening up, blossoming. In a strange way, role playing allowed her to be her true self when she was with him rather than the image she presented to the world. She wasn't Bettina Borlenghi, businesswoman and heiress. She was just Tina, a woman who wanted to love and be loved, like anyone else.

Luke knew her stay in New York was only temporary. He'd seemed willing to accept that. Maybe it suited him, too. She would try to make it up to him tomorrow. But why spoil their simple fun and fantasy with messy reality? Anonymity was her armor. She would wear it as long as she could.

Chapter Seven

The next day Luke closeted himself in his office at the back of the sports bar with the monthly accounts and tried to figure out how much money he could transfer from the bar's earnings to the foundation. His thoughts kept looping back to Tina, alternating between imagining a criminal past to account for her evasiveness and wishing she would waltz in and interrupt his day with another of her role playing fantasies. He'd never done these things with any other woman but he liked it—a lot. Sex with Tina was incredible.

He sighed and tried to drag his attention back to the accounts spread across his desk. He was hungry, and his stomach periodically made impatient noises, but he had to get this done before he took a break. The buck stopped with him. The foundation's employees, the kids, everyone was counting on him.

Rosie knocked on his open door and poked her head in. "A woman to see you, boss."

Speak of the Devil! Or should he say, an angel? Tina sauntered in, her long curling hair loose across bare shoulders. His gaze traveled down her body. Her fitted red sundress was gathered at the neckline by a yellow ribbon, nipped in at the waist and flared over her swaying hips. Wafting from the foil-covered tray in her hands came the delicious aroma of tomato and cheese.

"I found this Italian deli that makes fabulous home-made cannelloni. I thought you might like to try it." She set the package on his desk. "It's a peace offering. Don't be mad at me for yesterday, *per favore*."

How could he stay angry when she looked at him with those huge amber eyes? "Thank you, it smells awesome." He rose. "I'll get some plates from the kitchen."

"I would love to join you, but I have to go to work." She turned her head too suddenly and gave an audible hiss of pain. She rubbed her temples. "With a migraine."

"Let me." He came around his desk and pushed her hands away. Spearing his fingers through her hair he began to massage her scalp. After a night of getting knocked around the hockey arena in the old days he used to love getting massages and learned all the best spots to release tension.

She let her head drop forward. "Oh, that feels good."

"Late night?" She nodded. He worked his way down her neck, kneading her tight muscles. "If you're sick you should take a day off. My grandmother used to get migraines. She always said nothing helped as much as resting in a quiet, dark room."

Tina gave a soft, bitter laugh. "I wish."

His thumbs found the indentation at the base of her skull

and moved in firm circles. She groaned, halfway between pleasure and pain. "What time do you take your break? I'll come across and grab you. We could go for a walk."

"No, don't do that," she said quickly. "I'll probably work straight through today."

His fingers paused on the fragile stem of her neck. "Seriously, Tina. Your boss asks too much of you. It's not like you're getting a share of the profits."

"It's okay. I want to do it." She pulled away and gave him a grateful glance. "I'd better go."

He laid a hand along her cheek and bent to kiss her, angling his mouth for a stolen moment to taste and explore her lush lips and sweet tongue. He eased back and brushed her hair away from her face. "I'll call you later."

"*Sì*." She patted his chest and flashed him her brilliant smile.

His answering smile lingered long after she'd hurried out of his office. No doubt about it, she'd wriggled her cute curvy ass into his life and shimmied under his skin. So he'd buy into the fantasy. Enjoy it while he could.

Ask no questions, she'll tell you no lies.

• • •

Tina pressed her fingers to her forehead and tried to concentrate on what Janelle was saying. Along with Charmaine, they were seated around the coffee table in the office going over the inventory sold so far, trying to determine which articles were moving best in the American market. She'd taken pain relief tablets and Luke's massage had helped briefly but far from fading, her headache had intensified.

Through the window onto the showroom Tina could see customers browsing and Pam working the register while Kylie ferried garments to patrons in the fitting rooms and returned discarded clothing to the racks. The opening day sales were still on and bringing in plenty of business.

Janelle paused, her worried frown expressing concern. "Are you all right, Ms. Borlenghi? You look pale."

"I'm fine. And please, call me Tina." She smiled reassuringly through her pain and snuck at glance at her watch. They'd been at it for two hours. "Sorry, I missed the last thing you said. Could you repeat?"

Janelle tapped a column on the computer printout. "The evening gowns and lingerie are outselling the daywear. I've never seen that before."

"Is it the sale or the uniqueness of the designs?" Tina wondered.

"Why not expand the displays of those items and find out?" Charmaine suggested.

A commotion out in the showroom drew their collective gaze. Tina gasped, a hand to her mouth. "*Madre mia.*"

Fabio, flowing blond locks and male model handsome, had entered the store. He wore a black silk shirt and gold on his fingers and around his neck. He paused in the doorway, waiting until every eye was on him. His heavy Italian accent sounded clearly through the open office door. "Is Tina Borlenghi here? I wish to speak with her."

Tina surged to her feet and stormed out the door, leaving Janelle and Charmaine with open mouths. How dare he stroll into her store as if he owned the place? She would call the police. She would have him thrown out—

"Tina, *cara mia.*" Seeing her, Fabio held his arms wide

and came toward her.

She stopped dead behind the display counter. Everyone was now looking at her. Her hands clutched at the marble counter, her knuckles as white. She couldn't cause a scene. There were customers and employees present. She wouldn't let his presence hurt her boutique in any way, shape or form.

"Fabio." She managed a frozen smile that she hoped didn't give away how much she hated him. "What are you doing here?"

"I'm in town for fashion week, shooting the Calvin Klein collection." He reached out and caressed her cheek. "It's wonderful to see you."

It was all she could do not to strike his hand away. Switching to Italian, she kept her tone sweet to hide the vicious intent of her words. "You have ten seconds to leave my store or I'll call the police."

"But Tina," he replied smoothly, also in Italian. "I've done nothing wrong."

"You don't call lying, cheating, and swindling wrong? And now you're harassing me with a lawsuit." She wanted to spit in his plucked and exfoliated face. "You'll be laughed out of court."

"Ah, straight to the point. I always liked that about you. I've come to offer you a deal." He leaned on the counter and smiled pleasantly, his voice low and oily. "I know how you hate publicity, and you're so generous. You could save all the hassle by settling the matter beforehand. Two million Euros ought to salve my broken heart."

"You're not getting another penny from me!"

"What's the big deal?" He shrugged negligently. "That amount is nothing to you."

She wrapped her arms around herself in a vain attempt to stop shaking. This was a nightmare. Surely any moment she would wake up.

Charmaine and Janelle emerged from the office and stood behind her. "Is everything okay?" Charmaine asked, touching her shoulder.

"Everything's fine," Tina said with an effort.

"Like hell it is." Luke's voice sounded from the doorway. Then he was striding toward her, brushing aside curious shoppers to round the counter and put a supportive arm around her waist. "Tina, you're white as a sheet. What's going on? Is this guy bothering you?"

She clutched at Luke, grateful for his solid warmth beneath her palms and his imposing height and bulk at her side. She'd never been so glad to see anyone in her life. "It's okay. He can't hurt me. Not anymore."

Clearly not convinced, Luke turned to Janelle and Charmaine. He might not know who was the boss, but he was very definitive in his demands. "I'm taking her out of here. Look at her. She's been working way too hard. She needs a break."

"Wait a minute," Janelle said, shaking her head. "Who are you?"

"Luke Pederson," Charmaine said in something close to awe. "Is that your sports bar next door?"

"Yes," Tina answered. "He's my friend. I…I should take a break. Just for a few minutes."

"Take as long as you want." Janelle smiled. "You're the b—"

"*Grazie,*" Tina cut off Janelle in a rush. Ignoring Fabio, she tugged on Luke's hand. "Let's go."

• • •

Luke kept his arm tightly around Tina and led her across Madison Avenue against the traffic, hand upraised defiantly against the blaring horns and screeching tires, down another block to cross Fifth Avenue and enter Central Park. He took a side path through a shady byway, away from the nannies pushing strollers and the tourists studying maps. She was still trembling, and her face was very pale. He'd entered the store simply intending to see if she could go for a coffee but seeing her behind the counter looking ready to faint he'd seen red. All those women standing around with their mouths gaping, not doing anything to help. He wanted to punch something. Or some*one*, more like.

"Who was that guy?"

Tina was silent, as if trying to decide how to answer. They walked halfway to the lake before she finally spoke. "He's my ex-fiancé."

Fiancé. Not just boyfriend. Shit. What if Goldilocks wanted her back? Maybe they'd just had a fight, and he'd come to apologize. What if Luke had made a giant mistake dragging her out of there like some caveman? What if *she* wanted *him* back?

"You've got to give me more to go on than that." He stopped, forcing her to halt, too. "Come on, Tina. Talk to me. Do you still love him?"

"No!" She shook her head vehemently. "A thousand times no. I despise him."

Thank God. The strength of his relief surprised him. "What did he do to scare you?"

"He doesn't scare me." Color flooded back into her cheeks, and her hand shot out in an angry gesture. "I will not let him intimidate me."

"Good for you." Facing her, Luke took both her hands in his. "What did he want?"

"It doesn't matter now." When he started to protest she sent him a pleading glance. "I don't want to talk about it."

Luke couldn't let it go that easily. "He obviously upset you. Do you want me to kick his ass? I'd do it in a heartbeat. Just say the word."

"No!" She chuckled. "Although the offer is tempting. Thank you for taking me out of there. I almost expected to hear a bugle and see the Cavalry riding over the hill."

"If I could have arranged that, l'il lady, I would have." He pretended to tip a hat.

Tina laughed out loud, some of the sparkle returning to her eyes. Luke wrapped her in his arms and just held her, rocking her gently, stroking her back. She felt good, warm and soft. Safe. He was so glad she was with him and not that creep of an ex-fiancé. Then something occurred to him. "Did he follow you to New York? If he's stalking you, you should get a restraining order."

"It's nothing like that. I'm not in physical danger, I'm positive." Tina eased away. "He's a fashion photographer, here for fashion week. He must have looked for me once he arrived here, though." She pressed a hand to her chest. "Can we please not talk about him? It's such a lovely day and even though I should go back to the store I'm really enjoying just strolling through the park with you."

"Works for me." Luke turned down another path at random, wandering aimlessly to stretch this out as long as possible. Bees buzzed in the flower beds lining the path and out on the Great Lawn a yellow kite bobbed high in a clear blue sky.

Tina turned to watch a girl teeter past in red heels wearing skinny jeans ripped at the knees and a midriff-baring top. "I wish I had my camera. This would be a great opportunity to photograph some street fashion. Get a handle on what American women like."

"Do you want to be a photographer, or a fashion designer?" Made sense, if she did. She worked so hard, she was bound to be ambitious.

"Not a photographer." She plucked a leaf off a shrub and took a moment before replying. "Fashion design, yes. I've always loved the fashion industry. When I was a teenager I wanted to be a model." She shrugged. "I'm too...big for that."

She was sensitive about her weight, like so many women. He honestly didn't get why it would be an issue with Tina. Unless lover boy had made her feel bad about herself. Luke didn't often get an instant irrational hatred of a stranger, but he had the moment he'd seen Tina's stricken expression when confronted by that asshole.

"I'm glad you look like you do. It's why I'm so attracted." He pulled her into another hug, smoothing his hands down her back and over her nicely rounded ass. "I think you're perfect. And incredibly sexy." She opened her mouth to say something. He placed a finger over her lips. "Do you know what I like best about you? The way your smile lights up your whole face. It's like a small miracle every time."

Her wide mouth curved, lifting her cheeks and crinkling the corners of her shining amber eyes. Her light olive skin was smooth and clear. A warm glow seemed to emanate from within. Suddenly he was aware of his heart beating in his chest. "Yeah," he said gruffly. "That's what I'm talking about."

Tina stood on her toes and kissed him lightly on the lips. "*Tu sei molto dolce.*"

"I can see I'm going to have to learn to speak Italian." On second thought, how much could he learn in less than a week? He brushed away the thought before it could dim his good mood.

"I said you are very sweet." She slipped her arm through his elbow. "And now, I must go back to the boutique."

He went into the store with her, briefly, just to make sure dipshit had left. Then she walked him out again, standing next to the building out of the stream of pedestrians.

"I'm getting together with my old hockey teammates tonight to talk about the exhibition game but if your ex hassles you in any way, call me."

"I will, *grazie.* Maybe we can meet tomorrow after work?" She ran a hand up his shirt front. "You haven't told me what your sexual fantasy is."

"Hmm, let me think. Something prim and proper would be interesting. A teacher or librarian." He tugged lightly on the ribbon at her neckline. "Layers of clothing I could slowly strip away…"

"Ooh, I could get into that." Her full-throated laugh was full of promise. "I'll come to you this time…but you won't know when."

• • •

By the following afternoon, Luke was in a lather of antici-pation, waiting for Tina to arrive. As he sat at his desk, pre-tending to work, his niggling doubts about her crept back. Why would that man, her ex-fiancé, come to her workplace if they'd broken up? And why wouldn't she tell him what the guy wanted from her? The better he got to know her—and the more he cared—the more it bothered him that she wasn't open with him.

A knock sounded at the door. On cue, his pulse kicked up a notch. It had to be Tina because he'd asked Rosie and Luis not to interrupt him. "Come in."

Tina entered, wearing a trench coat. Her dark hair was scraped back in some tight, elaborate style. "Before we get started, I should let you know that I only have an hour."

"Okay." Now maybe he had a dirty mind but a trench coat on a woman shouted kinky to him. Underneath she would be wearing something hot and sexy. Leather or lace? Either would be good. "Did Rosie let you in?"

"No one knows I'm here." Tina pushed papers aside, sat on the side of his desk and crossed her legs. The neckline and hem of her coat gaped but all he could see were tanta-lizing shadows. "I slipped back here while the bartender was serving a customer. Your cook is chopping onions, and his eyes are too full of water to see."

"No more problems with your ex?"

She placed a finger across his mouth. "Shhh, we're not spoiling the mood by talking about him."

Luke nodded. Fair enough, but.... "You have an hour off in the middle of the afternoon." He slid a hand up her smooth calf then cut his gaze to hers. "Your boss isn't such an ogre, after all."

"No, she's actually a very nice woman." She studied him a moment, opened her mouth as if to say something, then seemed to think better of it. With a toss of her hair, she jumped to her feet. "Let's not waste time."

She turned her back to him and started unbuttoning her coat. All thoughts fled as his groin immediately tightened. Now the coat was hanging loosely, conjuring wild images of her sexy body. With her back still to him, she pulled a pair of severe black glasses out of her pocket and put them on. Oh boy. He gripped the arms of his chair, torn between the urge to rip the coat off and to wait to watch what would undoubtedly be a very sexy show.

Tina spun on her heel and flashed open the sides of her trench, letting it fall dramatically to the floor revealing a prim and proper black pencil skirt and demure blouse buttoned to her neck. The librarian or a teacher, he wasn't sure which. Didn't matter. Either way, her severe clothing couldn't hide her sexy curves any more than her cast down lashes concealed the glint in her eyes. Then she grabbed a yardstick leaning on his filing cabinet and slapped it against her thigh dominatrix-style. Fucking hell. He was rock hard, and he hadn't even touched her yet.

She paused, as if suddenly uncertain. "I shouldn't be here."

He tilted his head, unable to tell if she meant that for real, or in the game. With her hand not holding the yardstick she scraped at her thumbnail, a nervous gesture he'd noticed before. Suddenly the stakes felt very high. He chose his words carefully. "You must need me or you wouldn't have come."

"I've heard you know what a woman wants and how to

give it to her." Her smoldering gaze dropped and her voice became husky as she admitted, "I do need you." A pause and then, "That's not easy for me to say."

He stood and walked over to her. Took the ruler and propped it against his desk. He brushed his hand down her cheek, along her jaw to her slender neck to toy with her top button. Then he undid it. "You want to be exposed." He spread the collar wide. A pulse at the base of her neck fluttered. "You just don't know how to do it."

She cleared her throat. "You could show me."

"Oh, I'll show you." Every breath he took he drew in her scent, sweetly floral with earthy undertones, as complex as the woman herself. Warmth radiated from her and his body heated purely from proximity. "But you have to do what I say."

Holding her waist, he angled his mouth and kissed her, slowly, gently, coaxing a response. Teasing her full lips with his tongue till they parted and allowed him entry. Her hands crept onto his shoulders. Her breasts were near enough to brush his chest—close but not quite touching. It was as if they'd taken a step back from wild sex to exploration. It was surprisingly erotic. And scary. If she was afraid of being exposed he was equally terrified of wanting her so badly.

"I like it when you take charge," she breathed. "It's not easy always telling people to shush."

Librarian. That answered that question. He smiled against her mouth and edged closer so her breasts brushed his chest and their thighs touched. He heard her sharp intake of breath, and his cock stiffened. "I don't shush. I'm a badass hockey player. I do what I want."

She moved restlessly, pushing her hips forward till she

pressed against him. "You're too hot for a lady like me to handle."

He chuckled. "I bet beneath that uptight clothing you're a screamer." One hand spread across her ass, drawing her closer. The other hand reached for the clip holding up her thick mass of hair. "It's time you let your hair down."

Being firmly in role playing territory was almost a relief, but he felt a brief stab of disappointment at an opportunity lost for them to open up to each other. He released the clip and silky dark waves tumbled over his hand and down her back. Her chest rose and fell, making him itch to rip open the rest of her buttons. He made himself take it slowly, eke out the game by removing her glasses and tossing them on his desk. She blinked, looking suddenly defenseless. He had a powerful urge to take her in his arms and protect her.

Instead, he pushed back her hair and kissed her on the soft skin behind her ear. The heady scent of her skin made him lightheaded. Her lips found his ear lobe. She licked once then drew it in, sucking, making him think of her mouth on another, even more sensitive part of his anatomy.

"Getting bolder, are we?" he asked, his voice husky. "Let's see what's under that pretty blouse." He flipped open a button. And another. The rosy flush had spread down her neck and across her chest, tinging her lush breasts above a lacy red bra. His cock strained at the zipper of his pants. "What do we have here? The straight-laced librarian has a hidden naughty side to her. You're not such a good girl after all, are you?"

Her eyelids lowered. "I've been bad, actually. Really bad."

Was she admitting something? He decided to treat it

as part of the fantasy. "You *have* been bad. You need to be spanked."

She startled, glanced at the ruler leaning against his desk. "Is it really necessary?"

"With my hand." Jeez, he didn't want to actually hurt her. "Don't you want to go deeper, find out what how much fun being bad can be?" She nodded but her tongue darted out in a nervous lick to moisten her lips. "Don't be scared."

She raised her chin and met his gaze directly. "I'm not scared. I want you to do it."

"Then turn around."

Obediently, she turned and bent over the desk, pulling up her skirt till it was bunched around her waist, revealing skimpy red lace panties barely covering her smooth round ass. "Like this?"

For a moment, he couldn't find his voice. If he leaned forward he could move aside that scrap of lace and lick her... "No, I'm going to spank you on my lap." His hand itched to touch that silky olive skin, to see the red rise to the surface of her cheeks, to make her feel the sting...and love it. "Take the skirt off."

He pushed his chair out from the desk until he was backed against the filing cabinet. Still facing away from him, and saucier than any librarian *he'd* ever encountered, she slowly pulled down her zipper and pushed the fabric over her hips, bending to give him another mouth-watering view. Then she took off her blouse and positioned herself across his parted legs. A long stretch of bare flesh extended from her hips to her bra line, revealing the indentation of her vertebrae. She planted her elbows on his thigh, squeezing her breasts between her arms, then twisted her head to glance up at him with the sexiest smile he'd ever seen. "Do your worst."

He curved his palm around the ripe, fleshy mound of one cheek, feeling the rasp of lace and the firm, resilient flesh beneath his fingertips. Slowly, he moved his hand in a circular motion, enjoying the sight of the dark crevice between her cheeks opening and closing. His cock was painfully hard, his breathing shallow. Then without warning he raised his hand and brought it down sharply. *Smack.* A rosy blush spread in the imprint of his palm. She moaned a little and wriggled, moving her breasts against his thigh. It was almost unbearably erotic.

"Are you sorry for being a bad girl?" he said in a guttural whisper, blowing cool air on the hot slap mark and soothing it with his fingers. He was winging it now. Somehow their original game of "bad boy ruining the prissy librarian" had segued into her being the naughty one. He'd tried to stay in character, but the lust factor was taking over.

"I like being bad," she said, all low and sultry. Her accent was killing him. "I'm not sorry."

"Then I'm going to have to spank you again."

Taunting and sassy, she smiled at him, only her eyes visible over the luscious curve of her upper arm. Did it matter who she was in the real world when she was here with him, the sexiest woman he'd ever known? Whoever she was, she kept coming back for more. Giving it to her would be his pleasure.

He spanked her again, on the other cheek. She arched her back and then lifted her butt as if to give him better access. Again he struck, a bit harder, eliciting a gasp and then a sigh. He alternated between spanks and a light massage, getting a rhythm going until she was moaning in ecstasy, her eyes closed as she bit her bottom lip. When Luke was so turned on he couldn't take anymore he reached beneath her to unzip and give his aching cock some relief from the pressure of his pants. He stroked himself a couple of times and pushed the fingers of his other hand between her cheeks to find her slick, swollen folds. The head of his cock dragged against her bare belly, smearing a bead of liquid across her skin.

"Have you had enough, you bad girl?" His index finger circled her clitoris then dipped lower to enter her. She was so wet for him. And hot. And tight. He ached to be inside her, fucking her brains out. "Or do I need to teach you a lesson?"

She went still. "What kind of lesson?"

"First, call me, sir."

"Sirrrr." She dragged the last word out like a smart ass. Those rolled R's. Oh, God.

"I'm going to teach you to say please when you want something. I'm going to make you beg."

"Don't expect *me* to change *my* ways." Her tone was haughty, but her eyes held a spark of curiosity.

"Get up." He helped her to a standing position with her back to him, between his legs. His zipper was all the way down, his cock fully upright, hard and pulsing. "Bend over the desk."

Slowly, tantalizingly, she leaned forward and rested her elbows on the wood. He dragged her panties down to her ankles. She kicked them off and spread her legs. Her pussy was at eye level, ripe red and glistening. Tempting him to taste her. Gripping her butt he leaned forward and licked her, shooting his tongue forward to flick her clitoris. Her rear end swayed and lifted higher, giving him better access. He let go of her ass with one hand and found a breast, dragging her top down to expose the bare flesh to his touch. Caressing and molding, he squeezed her nipple to a hard peak as his tongue continued to tease, licking and circling till she was moaning.

"I want you inside me, Luke," she whispered. It was the first time she'd spoken his name through the whole exchange. It almost undid him.

His erection throbbed and the urge to plunge into her became almost impossible to resist. He fumbled in a side drawer on his desk for a condom and put it on. Then he stood up and positioned the head of his cock against her opening. "Tell me again, what do you want?"

"I want you inside me, fucking me." Her breathing was harsh, shallow.

He rubbed his cock back and forth in her groove, almost penetrating but then backing away before she could push back and take him in. "What do you say?"

"Please, Luke. Please fuck me."

"Now, my little librarian, I'm going to show you what you've been missing. You're going to love what I do to you." He gripped her hips and pushed into her, slowly and deliberately, savoring the exquisite sensation of stretching her and her gripping him, tight and hot as he penetrated deeper and deeper. He withdrew and did it again. He was at the ragged end of his control, more turned on than ever before in his life.

"Faster," she panted. "I'll be a good girl now."

"No, it's too late for that," he panted. "I'm going to fuck

you like you deserve to be fucked. The way you want to be fucked."

He started to pump, hard and fast. He was bent over her, his face buried in her hair, breathing her scent. One hand was splayed across her breasts, the other over her mound, forming a buffer between her and his pounding cock. With every thrust he pushed her clit against his fingers. She'd started out matching his thrusts but then his movement became too strong and now she braced her hands against the desk and held on.

"Oh, that's good. Yes. Yes." She was rocking against the desk. The desk legs banged on the carpeted floor. Papers slid off in a heap, pens scattered. "You make me feel so…good."

Just when he thought he couldn't hold on another second, she let out a half-shriek, half-moan and went limp in his arms. His whole body shuddered with one last, hard thrust and then he exploded into her, his hips pumping reflexively as he emptied himself.

Gently sliding out of her, he got rid of the condom and sank into the chair, pulling her onto his lap to wrap his arms around her. After the intensity of their lovemaking, speaking was too much effort. And unnecessary. Silently, she curled into him, soft and warm and compliant, and lifted her mouth to be kissed. Luke accommodated her in a long, luxurious melding of lips and tongues. Contentment seeped through every cell of his body. If he could have made this moment last an eternity he would have.

A knock sounded at the door. He sighed. Back to the real world.

"Luke, sorry to disturb," Rosie called through the closed door. "The liquor rep is here. Should I send him away?"

"I'll be out in a minute," he called to Rosie. "Give him a beer and tell him to sit tight."

"I have to go anyway." Tina pressed a final brief kiss to his jaw and started to unfold herself from his lap. Then she paused and tilted her head, regarding him seriously. "Do you…do this kind of thing a lot? The librarian, the cowboy…"

"Oh, you mean role-playing?" He chuckled and shook his head. Tenderly he tucked a strand of hair behind her ear. "You're my first time."

"Good." She gave a small, satisfied smile. "Me too." Then she rose and picked her trench coat off the floor.

Luke pulled his pants back up. "Are you free at six o'clock?"

"Um, possibly. Why?"

He pulled her back into his arms and pressed kisses to her temple. "I'd like you to see my kids play hockey. We have a game tonight. If we win this, we're through to the playoffs."

Her smile glowed. "I would love to see the *bambini*. Text me the address. I'll meet you there." She buttoned and tied her coat and finger combed her hair. "Don't come out with me. I'll sneak out the way I came."

She slipped out the door, and Luke released his breath. Whatever that role playing had really been about, there was nothing fake about her desire and her response to him.

Chapter Eight

Tina got Frank to drop her a block away from the hockey arena, just in case Luke happened to be outside when she arrived. She'd checked online to see what women wore to a hockey arena so she could blend in, not stand out. And while she was dressed too warmly for the muggy weather outside, once inside where it was a good twenty degrees cooler, she was glad of her cable knit cardigan, jeans, and boots.

She was supposed to be at a cocktail party, but her curiosity about Luke had won over her better judgment. She wanted to know more about the kids that meant so much to him. Plus she was curious about what he did when he wasn't working at his bar—or making her come her brains out.

Her butt still tingled pleasantly from his spanking. Just when she thought their passion couldn't get hotter, he ignited a flame that set her off like a rocket. Being in the public eye so much meant she rarely stepped "outside the box," but with Luke she was doing things she'd never tried with other men. Partly, her anonymity made her feel safe enough to be sexually daring, but mostly it was Luke himself. She loved that the things they did together were special to them. Her instincts told her he wouldn't hurt her.

On the other hand, her instincts had been wrong before. She really needed to remember that when she started getting sentimental about him. This afternoon in his office she'd been on the brink of telling him everything. Every word she spoke—and each of his replies—seemed to have double meaning. The lie was making her crazy with guilt, but the freedom to lose herself in sex play was intoxicating. Addictive. Now she worried that if she lost that ability to be so free she wouldn't be the woman he thought he was with, the woman he liked and lusted after.

She paused next to the concession stand and scanned the arena. Out on the rink, a man rode a big machine around, turning the roughened ice into a glistening smooth surface. The bleachers were dotted with parents and siblings, with more people arriving in a steady stream past the concession stand.

Luke was mid-rink, crouched before a group of boys about seven or eight years old in red and blue hockey uniforms. He wore a dark blue sweater over a white t-shirt and jeans with sneakers and his dark blond hair was ruffled. The children looked so small in their bulky padded uniforms, holding helmets and hockey sticks across their laps.

He glanced her way and raised a hand in greeting. Tina began to walk down to them on a hard rubber floor scored by thousands of ice skates. She stopped a few feet away so as not to interrupt his pep talk. Luke spoke to the children with passion, conveying his utter belief in their ability to win the game. And if not win, to play their absolute best. The kids gazed at him with rapt attention, with adoration, hanging on his every word, clearly inspired and determined.

Some weren't obviously disabled, but for others, their physical challenges were all too apparent. One boy with a shock of bright red hair and freckles sat in a wheel chair while another tall, blond boy wore metal braces on both legs. Another child with brown hair falling in his eyes clutched his padded gloves with short, malformed arms. There was a boy with Down Syndrome and one with eyeglasses so thick he had to be almost blind. The others she couldn't tell why they were on this particular team yet they must have had their own challenges. Her heart went out to them.

Moms and dads and siblings were clustered up and down the bleachers. A blond woman sat separate from the rest. Her chain store clothes were several years out of date and her boots worn and scuffed. But spread over the shoulders of her fleece jacket, beautifully pressed and artfully arranged, was a Borlenghi scarf in shades of green and gold.

Luke's sister, Stella. Her presence gave Luke another dimension, one at odds with his hot shot world of champagne and fancy restaurants. It was like looking through a peephole into a secret room in his life. What else was in there?

The children piled their hands on top of each other in the middle of the circle, chanted a cheer and then threw their hands up with a roar.

Stella shot to her feet and cupped her hands around her mouth. "Good luck, kids!"

Luke opened the gate that led onto the ice. "Okay, gang, skate a few laps and warm up. Michael, you're in goal. Timmy, practice your shots."

One by one, the kids clumped off the benches and onto the ice. The boy with the braces on his legs fell almost immediately but he got straight back up, given a hand by another child.

Tina drew closer to the group of parents, wondering if she should introduce herself to Stella or take a seat on her own. Before she could decide Luke came up to meet her, stepping over the wooden seats two at a time. He was clearly in high spirits, and he looked wonderful. The hair at his temples was damp and steam rose off his jersey, evoking the energy and athleticism of his old profession.

He kissed her cheek and then drew back, smiling. "You came."

"For you, every time," she said and winked. "You look happy."

"I always feel great when I'm at the rink with the kids. No matter what, they just keep trying. They're so inspiring." His proud gaze followed them moving awkwardly around the rink as if they were Olympic athletes and not children, some of whom could barely stay on their feet.

Tina nodded to the blonde. "Are you going to introduce me to your sister?"

"Sure. Come on." Taking her hand he led her over. "Stella, this is Tina. Tina, my sister."

"Pleased to meet you." Tina leaned in for her usual European kiss on both cheeks and then impulsively gave Stella a hug.

Stella blushed. "It's so nice to meet you. Luke told me all about you."

"Oh?" Tina raised an eyebrow at Luke. There wasn't that much to tell except for their sexual encounters. Surely he wouldn't confide those to his sister.

"I mentioned you worked at the boutique," Luke explained.

"He said you helped him pick out this scarf." Stella smoothed one corner proudly. "It's the nicest thing I've ever owned. Matches my eyes."

"I'm glad you like it." Tina turned to the rink. "Which is your son?"

"The boy in the wheel chair."

"Ah." Tina watched red-headed Timmy send a slap shot down the ice. "He's good." She turned back to Stella. "You must be proud of him."

"He's a little trooper, let me tell you." Stella's face lit. "He wasn't doing so well though until Luke started taking him out to the ice."

"Excuse me, ladies. I need to get back to my team," Luke said.

"Wait." Stella turned to her brother and lowered her voice. "Mom says she's been trying to call you, but you don't reply. I know you're still pissed but all that shit was a long time ago."

"Is it?" Luke's voice tensed up. "How can you be sure it's not still going on?"

Tina edged away and kept her gaze averted, but she couldn't help but overhear.

"It's her birthday," Stella continued. "Just call her."

"I'm not going to discuss this here." He leaned over and gave Tina a squeeze on the arm. "I'll catch up with you during the break." Then he ran down to the box.

"Sorry, family stuff. Have a seat." Stella patted the wooden bench next to her. "You a hockey fan?"

"I've never seen the game played live, but I'm looking forward to learning about it."

The other team came on the ice to warm up, and they were just as endearing as Luke's team, trying just as hard. The referee in his black and white striped shirt and black pants blew his whistle and dropped the puck on center ice.

Luke coached from the sidelines. Stella kept a running commentary, explaining what was happening play by play. The kids skated hard despite their handicaps. Tina winced every time they slammed into the boards. Once when Timmy and another boy in a wheel chair locked wheels after crashing into each other, the other boy got angry and started to raise his stick. Stella was on her feet in an instant, ready to go to her son's defense. Before the referee could even blow his whistle, Timmy said something that made the boy laugh and lower his stick. By the time Luke and the other coach had pried the chairs apart, the boys were chatting like best buds.

"Luke doesn't let the kids fight," Stella confided, sitting again. "Just because the pros do it is no excuse, he says."

"I understand Luke was really good when he played professionally," Tina said, then shamefacedly admitted, "I Googled him."

"He was MVP five years running and captain for six years," Stella said proudly. "Last year he was inducted into the Hockey Hall of Fame. He could have gotten a job coaching any top professional hockey team. Instead he chose to work with disabled kids, all because of Timmy. I'm a single mom, and he's like a surrogate dad to my boy. When Timmy's dad left us, I was working two jobs but Luke said, no, Timmy needed me. He helps me out so now I only have to work one job, during school hours."

"That's awesome." Family was of paramount importance to Italians, and Tina liked that Luke felt the same way. So it didn't make sense that he would neglect his mother. What was going on there? Not that it was any of her business...

Between periods Stella went off to talk to her son and pass around orange quarters for the kids to eat. Luke came up to sit beside Tina. He sat close and slipped an arm around her in a casual display of affection that was starting to feel normal and very welcome. "Enjoying the game?"

"*Sì*, I love the excitement. Stella is explaining all the plays. She says your team is behind. Do you still have a chance to win?"

"It's going to be close. We're only down by one point, but there's another period to go."

Luke hadn't repeated his demands to know her last name or where she lived lately. She should be glad he wasn't pressuring her, but for some perverse reason, she didn't like that he'd given up. Had he decided that he was fine with not knowing her, after all?

"I like your sister," Tina said. "She's lucky to have you for a brother."

"I go roller skating with her and Timmy in Central Park sometimes. You could come with us. If you wanted to, that is."

"I would love to." Then she remembered her killer schedule and her return flight to Rome. "If I have time. I have so much work to do and I'm not here for very long—"

"I know."

Her chin came up. "The launch of the boutique is important. I'm proud to be a part of it." She touched his arm. "But I will make time, I promise."

"I'd really like that." He glanced over his shoulder at the referee skating onto the ice. "I should get back to my team."

"Wait." She pulled him close for an emphatic kiss. "That's for being such a good brother." *Kiss*. "A good uncle." *Kiss*. "Coach."

He laughed against her lips.

"Luke, you are a very good man."

He pressed his lips to her brow. When he drew back, his gaze was so intense, so searching and…hopeful, she had to look away.

"I would like to buy the children something after the game," she said. "Hot chocolate or candy bars. Is that okay or would their parents object?"

"I'm sure the parents wouldn't refuse their children a treat. The kids would love it. Thanks, that's very generous of you."

Crazy loud organ music started up, signaling the game was about to recommence. Luke ran back down the bleachers to his team.

Stella returned to her seat next to Tina. "I hope the kids get a few goals. They win this, they'll make the quarterfinals. If they can keep playing, that is."

Tina dragged her gaze away from the rink. "You mean because of the financial problems of the foundation? I'm sure that will turn out okay."

"I hope so. Luke's working on fundraising. He's pretty stressed out about it."

Tina bit her lip. If she told him a million dollars would be in the bank in a matter of days he could relax. Now that she'd seen the kids play she was invested in their future. They had so little and deserved so much. Then she remembered Fabio and how his demands just kept increasing. She buried her face in her hands. This was nuts. Luke wasn't like that. She was becoming paranoid, riddled with doubts—about him, about herself, about what they were beginning to mean to each other. She could fall for him—if she let herself. But she couldn't. This was just a fling. Temporary.

"Hey, are you all right?" Stella asked, a hand on Tina's shoulder.

"Just…lightheaded. I didn't eat before I came."

"I'll get you a hot dog."

"No, but thank you. I'll be fine. I…just need some air." Fabio's lawsuit preyed on her mind. If Luke found out who she was, was he capable of blackmailing her for the money? Thank god he hadn't taken any photos of the two of them in compromising positions. Yet. Maybe that was coming. A man who wouldn't call his mother on her birthday… What kind of a man was that? Oh God. She'd just finished telling him what a good man he was. Now she could feel herself descending into panic and irrationality. She needed to get away so she could think clearly. "I…I should probably go."

The blare of a horn made her clap her hands over her ears. A red light flashed over the net and a point went up on the board. All the kids were crowded around Timmy's wheelchair, hugging him and cheering. Luke's team had scored. They were tied and now had a real chance to win. Fourteen minutes remaining. She bit a knuckle, so wishing she could see the joy on those kids' faces when—if—they won.

No, she had to go. Now while Luke was distracted by the commotion. Quickly she said good-bye to a bewildered Stella and made her way along the middle row of the bleachers, weaving in and out of parents on their feet cheering. She stopped at the concession stand and ordered hot dogs, hot chocolate and candy bars to be delivered to both teams after the game. Win or lose, all the kids deserved a treat.

Then she headed for the exit, texting Frank to come get her. She'd just slipped through the double doors to the unloading zone when Luke burst through after her.

"Tina, where are you going?" His puzzled gaze searched her face.

"I just remembered. I have a...meeting for the fashion show. Go back. You can't leave your team."

"The ref called a time out." He grabbed her hand, and she could feel the urgent tremor in his fingers. "You didn't mention a meeting before. You're running away again. Why?"

She shook her head, mute. There was no plausible excuse without going into detail about herself and her fears. The more she felt for him, the darker and scarier the fears became.

"I was hoping..." He paused and took a breath. "You would spend the night with me. No role playing—although I love that, don't get me wrong. But tonight I'd like it to be just about us, Tina and Luke. Could you do that? Is that possible?"

His words went straight to her heart. She wavered. Maybe he really did want her for herself. When he was standing right in front of her, so handsome and strong and yet in a way, also vulnerable, she wanted badly to give him the benefit of the doubt. Wanted to believe in him. In *them*. "Yes," she said slowly. "I can do that."

"Awesome." He pulled her into a huge hug and lifted her off her feet. "Now come back, please. Watch my team win."

"Okay." Out of the corner of her eye Tina saw the white limo turn into the driveway. Over Luke's shoulder she frantically waved Frank away.

Luke set her back on her feet and put his arm around her waist. As they turned to go he spotted the limo. "Wonder who that belongs to?"

"I wouldn't have a clue." Tina linked arms with him. "Come on. Your team will be wondering where you are."

They re-entered the arena as play was about to resume. Luke ran to rejoin his team. Tina followed at a jog, arriving in time to hear him say, "Okay, gang, we're going to pull the goalie and put six guys on. We need to score in these last few minutes. Timmy, Michael, Nathan, you know what to do. Get out there. Go, go, go!"

High over center ice, the clock counted down the final three minutes. To Tina it seemed impossible that the team would score a goal. There was so much fumbling of the puck and then the opposition got control and was heading down the ice toward the empty goal...

"*Per tutti i santi!*" Tina swore and prayed in Italian, jumping up to wave her arms. "*Forza ragazzi!*" Go children!

A shot went wide. Michael scooped it up behind the net and passed to Nathan who skated it up the rink. Timmy pushed his chair faster than anyone else could skate and was waiting near the goal. Stella was on her feet, yelling at the top of her lungs. Ten seconds. Tom shot it across the ice to Michael who passed it to Timmy. Timmy stopped it dead, did a quick spin of his chair and raised his stick. With a slicing motion, he slammed the puck toward the net. The red light went on a split second before the horn sounded the end of the game.

"He scored!" Tina jumped up and down, hugging Stella. "We won! We won!"

Luke ran up the bleachers to kiss her soundly. "You're our good luck charm."

Then she had to let him go congratulate his team. From the moment he returned to the kids, they crowded around him, clamoring and cheering. The parents came streaming down from the bleachers and joined the fun. Amidst all that, the concession delivered the food and drinks, and there was more cheering.

Luke smiled at her over the kids' heads, his gaze warm and loving. No role playing. Pretending to be someone else had been oddly liberating. Stripping aside her public persona had left her free her to connect with Luke on a physical and emotional level outside the "real" world. Now he wanted her to be just *her*. And yet he had no idea just who the real Tina was. Just as she certainly didn't know everything about him.

Pushing her lingering doubts aside, Tina met Luke's gaze and beamed back. He was worth taking a risk for. She wanted to trust him. Tonight maybe they would find out what they really felt about each other.

Chapter Nine

"There's a Thai restaurant around the corner," Luke said, surveying the meager contents of his fridge. The hot dogs and hot chocolate had gone down well with the kids, and Tina had been game to join in but he'd wanted to wait and give her something nicer.

"I've been eating out so much lately." Tina peered under his arm holding the fridge door open. "You have eggs, butter, cheese…" As she spoke she edged him aside and gathered the items. "I will cook for you. Where is your pantry?"

He slid out a tall thin door with narrow shelves containing jars of everything from anchovies to za'atar. He didn't even remember buying half of it. "You don't have to. Anyway, how can you make anything edible with what I've got?"

Tina placed the butter and eggs on the counter and picked out anchovies, olives and a package of flour. "My grandmother taught me how to make a tasty meal out of almost nothing. It's called *cucina povera*."

"I've heard of that. Peasant food, isn't it?"

"*Sì*." Tina dumped the flour onto the counter, made a hollow in the center and cracked in four eggs. "First, I make the pasta."

Bemused, Luke leaned against the counter. No one made their own pasta, not when even the corner grocery sold fresh tagliatelli. "I'll open some wine. Red or white?"

"Red, *per favore*." Within minutes she'd mixed up the dough and was putting it in the fridge. "Now we put her to bed for a little rest."

He drew the cork from a bottle of Trebbiano and poured them each a glass. "While 'she's' resting we could go to bed too."

She gave him a stern look that reminded him of the librarian with her ruler. "No, now we prepare the sauce. I must feed you before I take you to bed." She handed him a block of parmagiana. "You can grate the cheese."

"Yes, ma'am." Luke grated while Tina chopped garlic, anchovies and chili and dropped them into sizzling olive oil. "When I was a kid we had our own form of peasant food. Packaged mac and cheese with fried bologna. It's not bad if you don't know any better."

"Tell me about your childhood." Turning the frying pan down low, she took the dough from the fridge and started rolling it out.

"Three kids and three adults in a three bedroom house. You do the math. Stella and my grandmother shared. I bunked with my brother. You don't know the meaning of stink until you stuck your head into a bedroom shared by two teenage boys."

Tina wrinkled her nose. "I do know. I have—had—two

brothers."

"Had?"

"My oldest brother died in a car accident in his early twenties." Her mouth turned down as she pushed the rolling pin across the dough in swift strokes. "My father died the same year from a heart attack." Abruptly she stopped rolling.

"Hey, I'm sorry." He pulled her into a hug. She turned her face into his chest and took a deep, shuddery breath. He stroked her back and she relaxed. "Okay?"

"*Sì*." She eased away and dabbed at her eyes. "It was years ago, but I miss them so much. If I could go back in time I would take back every harsh word, every fight we had. Life is too short, and family is too important to be apart."

Luke went back to grating cheese. Her words were too pointed to be anything but deliberately chosen. The silence seemed to stretch. "You overheard my conversation with Stella about our mom."

"I couldn't help it. I know it's none of my business but…" She paused. "Do you have a large pot to boil water?"

He found one in a bottom cupboard, filled it at the sink then put it on the stove to heat. Tina added a can of chopped tomatoes to the frying pan then continued to roll the pasta, pushing it out at the edges.

Finally Luke sighed. "My mother has a gambling problem. When I was a kid she lied constantly to cover up her actions and how much money she spent. Plenty of times we didn't even have mac and cheese to eat. When I was eight, on the eve of my first hockey playoffs, she pawned my new ice skates to play the slots. I had to call a friend and borrow a pair. It was so embarrassing." The pain in his chest even after all these years made it hard to speak the next words.

"The worst part was, she missed my big game, after promising she'd be there."

"Oh," Tina said softly. "That's bad."

He'd looked for her in the stands repeatedly through the night. After he made a goal. When his team won. Finally it had dawned on him. She'd never intended to come.

"That's just one example. I could give you dozens more," he said bitterly. "It's a disease, I understand that, but she let the family down over and over with her lies and cover-ups. She would swear to my dad she was getting counselling and then use the money to gamble. Often we didn't find out the truth until it was too late, and then the electricity would be cut off or we'd go to school without notebooks and pens."

"I see," Tina said, even more quietly than before. She took a knife and started cutting the pasta into long thin strips.

"She sold my dad's prize vintage Mustang convertible that he'd spent years restoring. He went away for the weekend on a fishing trip. When he came back it was gone, sold to some asshole off the street for a fraction of its real value."

"How could she do that? Cars are registered."

"Nobody cares about that on the black market. That's when we realized how low she'd sunk, that she had seedy connections none of us knew about. That's when I decided the only way to deal with her was tough love. I help her out with living expenses, and she'll always have a roof over her head, but other than that, she's not part of my life."

Tina put down the knife and clasped her arms with her floury hands, shivering as if he'd just said he was cutting *her* out of his life. "Has it worked?"

He shrugged. "I don't know. I never know what I can

believe. There's so much dirty water under the bridge, frankly, I don't care anymore."

"But she's your mother, and it's her birthday." Tina finished cutting the last few pieces of pasta. "Stella's right. You should call. Or someday when it's too late you may regret it."

Did she think he didn't regret it now? He missed his mom for all her faults. There had been good time, times when she'd been loving and warm. But he was still angry. He didn't think he could bear to hear another lie coming from her lips.

"What about the rest of your family?" he said, changing the subject. "You mentioned a brother who likes football. Do you have sisters?"

"Two. Francesca is in furniture and Angela works in fine food. Angela is an amazing cook. It's a shame she isn't here right now." Tina gathered up the pasta strips, dusted them with flour and swirled them into a loose ball.

"You're not doing too badly." Her sister might be the expert, but Tina was no novice in the kitchen. He lifted the grater and uncovered a mound of fine cheese shavings. "And your brother?"

"He's the head of a company. He helped put Angela through cooking school and paid for Francesca to take business courses. He helps me too, in many ways."

"So, no more *cucina povera* for your family."

She flashed him a quick glance. "No."

"What about your mother? Does she work?"

"She's very family-oriented," Tina said and smiled. "Mamma sees her main job as giving advice to her children. Sunday lunch everyone has to come together. We spend a summer holiday together, too, in Naples."

"And go to the soccer game."

"*Sì*." She grinned. "We love our football."

Luke was forming a picture of a close-knit family, struggling to overcome what must have been a devastating blow when Tina's father and brother died. But they'd worked hard, supported each other and bettered themselves. He could imagine her growing up in one of those tall terracotta-colored houses with clothes hanging on the line and kids playing below in the street. Her mamma cooking vast pots of pasta for a large, extended family.

"I have my own place," Tina added, dashing that romantic and probably stereotypical notion. "I adore my family, but I need my own space."

"Do you have any nieces or nephews?"

"Not yet. But my brother married recently so I'm hoping there will be a *bambino* in the near future." She carried the pot to the stove to heat.

Luke refilled their wine glasses. "Are your sisters married?"

"No, they're single, much to my mother's sorrow. Angela is the youngest. I think she might be romantically interested in someone, but she's denying it. As for Francesca…" Tina shrugged. "I don't know if she'll ever settle down. At one time, she planned on becoming a nun until she discovered boys."

"Three girls. Your poor brother."

"With Giorgio's wife Layla, we feel as if we have a fourth sister. But he knows we all adore him. Believe me, he can take care of himself."

"Do you get lonely in New York?"

"I miss my family, but I haven't had time to be lonely."

She glanced up at him through her lashes. "I've had you."

For as long as it lasts. The unspoken thought hung in the air between them. Luke put his wineglass down and drew her into his arms. He kissed the spots of flour on her nose and cheek and tucked back the lock of hair falling out of the knot she'd pinned to the top of her head. He hadn't intended to get busy right away, but she felt so good and her mouth was warm and welcoming, familiar yet still excitingly new. He started to unbutton her jeans.

"I thought you wanted an evening that wasn't just about sex," she murmured between kisses.

"When I get near you, my body has other ideas. Seeing you in my kitchen, making me a meal…it's very sexy."

"Everything is sexy to you! I have to finish cooking. Never come between an Italian and food." She softened her scolding with a smile. "Can you can set the table?"

"Sure." Luke carried pasta bowls and cutlery into the dining area. In the kitchen, Tina moved from sink to stove, her thick black hair misting from the steam of the pots. He admired her competence and independence, but he also appreciated this glimpse of her nurturing side. He couldn't recall the last time a woman had cooked a meal from scratch for him.

He hated that she'd been hurt by some asshole. Every time he remembered the vulnerability in her eyes that first day when she'd asked him if he thought she was attractive he wanted to hit something. How was it even possible for her to doubt that? He wished he could take care of her so she didn't have to work such long hours. Lavish on her the finer things in life she appreciated but mostly couldn't afford.

He put on soft music and dimmed the lights. Tina carried

the food to the table and dished him a plate of simple but delectable pasta.

"You're an awesome cook." He wound the *al dente* strands onto his fork along with cheesy sauce flecked with herbs. "Your ex-fiancé's loss is my gain."

She tensed, her fork pausing mid-air. "I don't want to talk about him."

"I didn't mean to bring up bad memories, only to compliment your cooking." He had to admit though, he was curious about her ex. Had he put her off relationships completely? "Are you only interested in flings? Do you ever intend to marry?"

A hint of humor glinted in her large amber eyes. "Are you proposing?"

"Would you say yes?" he teased back, wondering at himself for pursuing this line of conversation. Sure, one day he would marry and have a bunch of kids, but for now he enjoyed his bachelor freedom.

Her reply was nothing if not oblique. "You're still a celebrity even though you don't play hockey anymore. That lifestyle can be difficult. Dealing with the paparazzi, the intrusions into your private life, not knowing who to trust… "

"It has its perks. When you love what you do, you put up with it."

"*Sì*, but there's always a price to pay."

The bitterness in her voice surprised him. Had her ex been a man with a high profile for whom the demands of his lifestyle meant the relationship was always relegated to the background? Impulsively he laid a hand over Tina's. "But you're down-to-earth. The real deal. I love that about you."

Shadows clouded her expressive eyes, and she dropped

her gaze. "You don't really know me that well."

"I would like to." He leaned forward, gripping her hand tighter. "Have you considered staying in New York and working full time at the boutique? I bet they'd have you in a flash."

"You don't know the situation. It's not that easy."

"But wouldn't you like to? A new store would be bound to have opportunities for career growth. With your smarts you'd advance quickly." He winked. "Think of all the role playing fantasies we could explore."

"It's not possible." She got up and carried the empty plates to the kitchen, signaling the conversation was over.

Undeterred, Luke followed her. He touched her chin and turned her face to his. "What did he do to you that makes you so afraid you can't even tell me your last name or where you live? I'm not going to hurt you."

She searched his face as if looking for a guarantee. "I thought he loved me. Turned out he was only using me. I couldn't believe I was fooled so completely. Love made me blind, but I won't make the same mistake twice."

Was she telling him not to expect anything from her? She'd made it clear from the beginning their affair was only temporary. He'd been down with that. And yet, to hear her say "never" as she looked at him set off a dull ache in his chest. Which was dumb. His team and his family provided all the warm fuzzies he needed.

But it would be a tragedy if a woman as warm and loving as Tina, a woman to whom family was so important, never found the love she deserved.

"Never say never." He reached for her and pulled her into his arms. If they couldn't have love, they could at least give each other comfort. "Enough talking for one night."

The kiss tasted bittersweet, full of the longing and yearning neither of them could repress. That their time together was limited made it all the more precious. The thought of letting her go, it opened up something inside his chest.

He loved her.

Luke hadn't meant to fall in love, and yet now that it was happening he was powerless to stop himself. The epiphany wasn't earth shattering or even much of a surprise. The signs were there all along. His intense attraction to her, the way he thought about her all the time, the way she made him laugh, the powerful feelings of protectiveness she inspired in him...

When he took her to bed, there was no role-playing. Even though she hadn't told him much more about herself than he knew before, the way she kissed him so sweetly and so urgently was genuine. Tenderly, he removed her clothing, piece by piece, taking time to kiss and caress each newly exposed part of her body, as if to show how much he valued her. Cherished her. Loved her. She did the same for him until they were both stripped naked in the near dark.

He lay side by side with her, gazing into her face. Touching her smooth skin, his fingertips trailing a long, curving path from cheek to collarbone, from breast to smooth belly, brushing the long muscle of her thigh to find the tender skin behind her knee. He'd never known anyone to be so perfect.

They didn't speak a word. Instead they communicated with their eyes and their hands, their lips and tongues. The slide of hips between parting thighs, and mouths entangling. He entered her slowly, hyper-aware of every flutter of her eyelashes, every beat of her heart, every pulse of her blood beneath her skin. She came moments before he did, just enough time for him to experience her bliss before he imploded.

Tonight she made no objection to staying, just snuggled under the covers and folded herself around him, her soft breath fanning the hairs on his chest. Luke stared up through the skylight at the stars peeking through shifting clouds and held her. Today and tonight, had been different. The thing was, he didn't know if it marked the beginning of something new—or the end of their affair. Had he convinced her that love was worth taking a risk for? Or was she saying good-bye in her own sweet way?

As usual he had more questions than she had answers. But this was the most perfect night together so far. If it was the beginning of the end, he didn't want to spoil it.

Luke gathered her closer, his chest aching and filled with turmoil. If only they could stay this way forever, holding each other close, safe from the intrusions of real life. Not just for a week but for years and decades, for all of their lives.

Chapter Ten

Tina drowsily opened her eyes and stretched luxuriously. She'd had such a good sleep, the most rest she'd had since coming to New York. Early morning light filtered through slate blue blinds. She reached for Luke. But his side of the bed was empty. She sat up and looked around. There was a note on his pillow.

Gone to pick us up some breakfast. Back soon.

She flopped back down with a dreamy sigh. Last night had been beautiful. Cooking for him, eating their simple dinner together, hearing about his family and his past hockey triumphs. His story about his mother touched her deeply. Her heart ached for both mother and son, and for the whole family. But she admired Luke all the more that he'd overcome personal disappointments and the loss of his career and poured all his energies into building something that mattered for kids who had so little. That was the mark of a really special man.

Their love-making had been profound and moving, a true emotional connection far more satisfying than role-playing. To have both with one man seemed a miracle. She was falling in love with him. Perhaps she was already there. *Never say never.* He'd been right, and sooner than she could have imagined.

He'd said he only wanted a fling, but she didn't believe it. Not after last night. Maybe it was too early to talk about a lasting relationship, but that's where they were headed.

A horn blared outside on the street, startling her out of her rose-tinted dream. There would be no such thing as a lasting relationship while she was lying to him. She needed to tell him the truth about who she was. But how could she, after what he'd said about his mother and how he felt about people who lied? He would be furious. If he couldn't even forgive his own mother how would he ever forgive her?

Anxiety tightened her chest, and she rolled over, twisting the sheets around her. She had to get through the fashion show. After the boutique's opening day, it was the biggest event on her agenda during her trip to New York. It was why she was here. She couldn't allow herself to forget that. If she failed in launching the House of Borlenghi in America after all the hard work to convince Giorgio to let her and her sisters run their own businesses, she'd be in the same boat as Angela, struggling to prove herself. She'd come too far to let that happen.

She glanced at the bedside clock. Nine-thirty a.m. *Madre Mia!* She was supposed to be at the dress rehearsal for to-night's fashion show half an hour ago. Throwing back the covers she bounded out of bed, reaching for her clothes. She couldn't leave until Luke came back but there would be no time for breakfast. Hopefully he would understand.

• • •

Luke whistled as he strode down the street to his favorite deli to pick up coffee and bagels, weaving effortlessly through pedestrians hurrying to work and tourists out bright and early for sightseeing. Cars and trucks clogged the street, taxis nosed their way through, buses rumbled past. He smiled at a little boy tugging on his mother's sleeve. All the colors seemed brighter this morning, the sky bluer, the leaves on the trees surrounded by little iron picket fences, greener. He could even hear a bird twittering somewhere.

He pushed through the glass doors and stood in line at the bakery counter. He'd just placed his order when an extra-long honk made him glance out the window. A bus had just pulled into the bus stop out front. Whatever traffic snarl had caused the honk was instantly forgotten when he got a look at the ad on the side of the bus. *What the fuck?*

Larger than life was a photo of Tina, all wide, white smile and wavy dark hair, wearing a spangly red evening gown, lying on her back with one high-heeled foot kicking in the air. The caption read, House of Borlenghi. *Veni, Vidi, Vici.*

The buxom forty-something woman in a floral smock behind the counter plunked down his paper sack and carry-out tray of coffee. "That'll be twelve-fifty." Then she noticed him staring at the bus. "That's the owner of the latest *It* boutique. She's pretty hot stuff, huh?"

"The *owner*?" Luke blinked stupidly. The bus doors closed on new passengers and with a belch of black diesel smoke, pulled back into traffic.

"Yeah. I heard her talking on the radio the other morning. Italian dame. Betty Borlenghi." The woman frowned and blew back wispy brown bangs with a huff of breath. "Somethin' like that. Betty doesn't sound Italian, does it?" She shrugged it off. "Did you want somethin' else, mister?"

"No, thanks." Luke handed over a ten and a five. "Keep the change."

Back on the sidewalk he stared after the bus slowly inching through morning rush hour. Betty? Maybe the woman in the deli had the name wrong but there was no doubt the face on the bus advertisement was Tina's. *Salesgirl, my ass. She was the goddamn owner of the boutique.*

Veni, vidi, vici. He might not speak Italian, but he knew that Latin phrase. *I came, I saw, I conquered.*

She'd done that all right. She'd sure had him going—up, down and sideways. All the while she'd had him thinking she was a sales assistant. Had she been laughing at him? Did it amuse her to fool a man so completely?

And how about her tale of woe about being used by her ex-fiancé? Luke felt pretty used himself. Acid churned in his stomach and burned the back of his throat. Had she ever planned to tell him the truth? What did he really know about her? As he'd told Allan, he only had a handful of facts. How many of those were actually true? Did she have a brother who'd died? Did she have more siblings? Did she even live in Italy? He didn't know what to believe about her anymore.

A passerby jostled him, and he shook his head, coming back to the busy sidewalk. Mechanically, he retraced his path back to his apartment half a block away. With every step the hard knot in his gut twisted tighter. Why hadn't she wanted him to know who she was? She must think he was good enough to screw but not good enough to be part of her real life.

As she'd said herself, she was here for a good time, not a long time.

He tucked the sack of bagels under his arm and, juggling the coffee tray, pulled out his phone and Googled the House of Borlenghi with his free hand. The New York boutique was only the latest expansion of the Italian fashion empire founded by Bettina—Tina—Borlenghi. There was a photo of her wearing a power suit with her hair tamed into a sleek ponytail, in a group with other bigwigs of the European fashion scene. Clicking a few more links took him to the parent company, the Borlenghi Group. It was in the Fortune Five Hundred and had thousands of branches and subsidiaries all over the world.

Fuck me dead. Luke walked on, dazed. He might be good at getting a woman to take off her clothes, but when it came to the fashion world, he was clueless. No doubt she'd counted on his ignorance to get away with her deception. His fist tightened around his phone as he thought back to the first day. *I'll be anything you want me to be.* Had she been playing him all this time? Stringing him along, thinking what a fool he was for believing that one of the richest women in the world was a salesgirl? Well, what else was he supposed to think when she was dressing a mannequin? Who did that when they had literally thousands of employees to call upon?

His phone rang. His heart began to race thinking it might be her. But it was Allan. "Hey, bro." He couldn't hide the tremor of outrage in his voice.

"What's up? Are you all right?" Allan asked. "You sound strange."

"I…" Shit. He needed to have this out with Tina before he went spilling it all over town. On the other hand, before he went batshit crazy at her maybe he should have someone talk him down from the ledge. "I just found out Tina's last name. Borlenghi. I saw her face on a fucking bus."

Not just her face, her whole luscious body. Was that part of what rankled? Here he'd thought he had his own sweet salesgirl all to himself. Now he found out she belonged to the world.

"Holy shit," Allan said. From his tone Luke surmised he must already be Googling her. "So all this time she's secretly been a billionaire heiress. Have you seen the family yacht in Naples? This is awesome, dude."

Yacht. Of course. Not a yak or a yurt or a yellow submarine. Was he dumb or what?

Awesome? "Are you kidding me? She lied, man. Lied straight to my face." A thousand painful memories from his childhood surged forth, made him jerk his hand and spill coffee down his pants. Disgusted, he tossed the whole tray, cups and all, into a nearby trash can. "Have you forgotten what my family went through with my mother?"

"Right, of course." Allan immediately sobered. "Yeah, Tina did kind of screw you around, didn't she? Why did she do that?"

"I don't have a clue. I'd better go. She's at my apartment, and I'm bringing back fucking bagels for breakfast in bed." His stomach hurt all over again at the thought of the scene to come.

...

Tina paced the kitchen. She'd already texted Frank to pick her up, now she was texting Charmaine to let her know she would be late. She had her shoes on and her handbag slung over her shoulder.

Charmaine's reply pinged back seconds later. *Big glitch! Venue double booked. Could lose out to Donna Karan. Lincoln Center manager insists on talking to you!!*

No, no, no, this couldn't be happening. Where was Luke? She had to leave right now. She opened the door and glanced down the hall toward the elevator. She went back inside and paced some more. Sent another text to Charmaine asking her to get the manager to call her.

Luke's key turned in the lock. He entered, scowling. A huge coffee stain extended from his thigh below his knee.

"There you are," Tina cried. "Thank God. I'm so sorry. I have to go. I'm late."

"So what else is new?" There was an uncharacteristic coldness in his voice. He tossed down the paper bag in his hand so hard it slid across the marble counter and fell on the floor.

Tina put a hand to her gold necklace. The deep freeze permeated his eyes, too. Something was dreadfully wrong. Then she realized the truth evident in every cold hard line of his face and body. *He knew.* Somehow, in the half hour he'd been gone, he'd found out her identity. Her instinctive reaction was to go into denial. "W-what is it, Luke? What's wrong?"

"Why don't *you* tell *me*? Isn't there something you'd like to say to me…Bettina? Or should I say, *Signora* Borlenghi? I suppose that's your limo downstairs. You must have been slumming it that day you took a taxi to the St. Regis."

Her throat went dry. She was falling, sinking through the floor, the walls closing in on her. Her mouth opened but she couldn't speak. Somehow though the words croaked out. "H-how did you know I'm staying at the St. Regis?" A tiny curl of indignation penetrated the thick fog of guilt and regret. "Did you *follow* me?"

Luke's blue eyes were icy but below the surface a storm was brewing. "You wouldn't tell me a damn thing about yourself. What was I supposed to do?"

"Trust me?" She'd meant it to come out stronger but her voice cracked on "trust." She cleared her throat and straightened her shoulders. This day was already spiraling out of control. She absolutely could not break down.

"Oh really, the way you trusted me," he said flatly.

"I never meant to hurt you." Her heart beat erratically but she managed to keep her voice even. "We were having a fling. You agreed that it was only temporary. I was just casual sex to you."

He threw her a scathing glance, and she was forced to step out of his way as he bulldozed past her into the dining area. "You were *never* just sex to me. Why did you lie about who you were?"

She clenched her hands to stop them from trembling. "I intended to tell you, I really did. But when you assumed I was a sales assistant, going along with it just seemed easier. If you knew who I was, you would have acted differently around me."

"Oh, you mean I would be scheming to get my hands on

your money," Luke said, disgusted.

"No. Yes." She gestured impatiently. "Okay, I might have thought so in the beginning, but that was before I got to know you."

"Did I *ever* ask you for a single dime?" he snapped.

"No, but Fabio—"

"Fabio's an asshole."

"He pretended to love me only to further his career. He's still asking me for money."

"*I'm not Fabio.*" Luke ground out the words so harshly she wanted to cover her ears.

"I know that now, but I didn't at first. In the beginning, I didn't think we would last. You didn't, either. But after a while, I wanted to get to know you. That's why I came to the hockey game. And last night? That was wonderful." She dabbed at her eyes. "How can you turn your back on that? I wish…"

She wished for lots of things. Trust, first and foremost. Love. Fireworks. Ordinary things like hockey games and roller skating in the park. Oh, she would never give up House of Borlenghi. She'd created the atelier and built it into an international business. Why did it seem so impossible for her to have both the privileges that came with success and a lasting relationship?

Luke moved restlessly, pacing the perimeter of the carpet that covered the hardwood floor almost to the wall. "You should have told me the truth, if not right at the beginning, then soon after."

"Yes, I should have. But now that you know about Fabio, y-you could forgive me."

Her plea fell into a profound silence. He wasn't going to

dignify her plea with a reply. Some of her hurt turned to anger that he could just leave her hanging. With every second that ticked past, her heart hardened a little more. "Okay, if that's the way you want it."

She got a leather folder out of her handbag and wrote a check. The money had gone into her account yesterday and now that Luke knew who she was there was no point in sending the donation anonymously. She slid the check across the dining table. "That's for the foundation."

"I don't need your money, thanks very much."

"It's not for you. It's for the kids."

He planted his hands on the table and leaned forward. "Did you hear what I said? I. Don't. Want. Your. Money. You can't buy me."

She stiffened, drew back her shoulders. "I wasn't trying to."

He looked at the amount on the check, and his mouth tightened. "Buy me off, more like."

She watched his face for any sign, even the smallest, that he felt anything for her. "Why can't you accept my donation? You were going to when you thought I was a salesgirl."

Picking up the check he circled around her. "I would have taken an honest fifty dollars from you but not a guilty million. We're through."

"Were we ever really together?" Tina asked bitterly. "You clearly care nothing for me. It really was just a fling. By turning down my money you make me feel used in a different way. Fine for sex but not for anything that matters."

"Now you know how *I* feel."

She stared at him. How could they both have it so wrong? "Don't tear up my check. We have to put aside our differences for the children's sake."

"And have you always wonder if I used you? No way." He shook his head. "Admit it, Tina, you would never be with a guy like me long-term. Our lives would never have meshed. I was fine for sex games, but there was no point in telling me who you were because that would mean letting me into your real life."

Oh, god, they were accusing each other of horrible things. Wrong things. For a few minutes, she'd had a crazy hope that they could talk this out and make up. That they would fall into each other's arms, laughing about what a silly fight they'd had. Instead their explanations turned into mis-interpretations that seemed to push them farther apart.

"I-I should go." Maybe if she wasn't here, he would cool down and come to his senses about keeping the donation.

"Tina, you're an amazing woman who any guy would be proud to be with. Why do you think you need to give a man money to earn his love?" He waved the check. "Soon as I've destroyed this, you can go. You'll never have to see me again. That's what you want, isn't it?"

No, her heart cried.

Let him go, countered the voice of painful experience.

Without further warning Luke tore the check in half. She winced, as if he was tearing her heart in two. The pieces of paper fluttered to the floor. She and Luke were through, that was clear. What was true and real between them had been destroyed by too many lies, too many games.

A horrible clarity pervaded her mind as she realized he would never, ever forgive her. No matter how much she begged or pleaded or tried to explain. The cruelly ironic twist to his mouth told her he'd heard it all before. From other women. From his mother. Tina could choose between humiliating herself by groveling at his feet or salvaging the American launch of the House of Borlenghi.

She drew herself up with as much dignity as she could muster. "I have business to attend to."

On shaky legs, she crossed the dining area and went down the short hallway and out the door. One foot in front of the other, all the way to the elevator. Her eyes were pricking hard, but she didn't look back, didn't break stride. She stabbed the button and breathed a sigh of relief when the doors parted.

He didn't call her back. Or utter one word to soften their good-bye. *Va bene*. He was cruel, no better than Fabio.

Riding down to the lobby, her hurt segued into righteous indignation. How dare he treat her as disposable? Had this last week, especially last night, meant nothing to him, allowed her no benefit of the doubt in his mind? Clearly not.

She slipped into the limo. "*Buongiorno*, Frank. Lincoln Center, *per favore*."

Anger was empowering.

She strode into the tent set up outside the Opera House at Lincoln Center. The normally unflappable Charmaine and the hapless booking officer were both nearly in tears. Tina took one look at the manager, a sweaty, round-faced man in his forties, and tore strips off him. If she was such a terrible person she would make it work for her. Within ten minutes he was apologizing profusely and promising her that the venue was hers exclusively.

The rehearsal went ahead on schedule, but there were problems. A fight had broken out with a fashion editor and a top fashion blogger over who got the last reserved seat in the front row. One of the models had come down with the flu and the casting agent had snagged a super model, but she was demanding double her usual pay rate. There was a glitch in the air conditioning and the event manager was waiting for the technician. Fingers crossed it would be fixed by show time.

With the rehearsal over she went back to her hotel. It would have been nice to collapse, but she didn't have the luxury when there was work to be done. First, a phone interview with the fashion editor of the New York Times. Then a few tweets to her new American followers about the fashion show. A Facebook update and photos posted to Instagram. She made a call to Janelle to see how the shop was doing and then checked in again with Charmaine to discuss the final arrangements.

Finally she'd dealt with everything that was in her power to deal with and tried to force the rest out of her mind. While she prepared for the show she flipped on the twenty-four hour news channel, but the events of the world washed over without penetrating. She knew she should eat something, but she had no appetite. Losing Luke was like a black hole, sucking all the joy out of her life. She couldn't wait for the fashion show to be over so she could get out of New York and go back home to Rome.

She hated that he'd torn up her check. What was going to happen to the *bambini* if they couldn't play hockey? Yes, she knew he had fundraising on the go, but she wanted to help, too. If only there was a way she could contribute in a way that didn't come from her personally, a way that Luke wouldn't be able to turn down.

The fashion show. That was it! She called Charmaine

and asked her to track down Stella's phone number. Her agent called back with it within minutes, and Tina placed the call. It would be so great to turn the event into more than just business and at the same time make up for the loss of her donation.

"Stella," she said when the other woman answered. "I know this is horribly last minute but I have an idea to raise money for the foundation. I'm hoping you can help me out."

She chatted to Stella for half an hour, taking care not to let on that anything was amiss with her and Luke. Any sympathy at this point, and she might dissolve in a flood of tears. His sister would only find out they'd broken up when Tina was long gone. There would be time enough to cry when she was back in Rome.

With every item crossed off her "to do" list, Tina took a long shower, did her hair and makeup and then put on her red sequinned gown, the one she'd posed in for the bus ads. It had become something of a signature look for her in New York, part of her brand. Really, it was a wonder Luke hadn't come across a photo of her before today.

She smoothed on concealer beneath her puffy eyes. She couldn't bear for even Frank to know she'd been crying. And her family would be there tonight. They would ask questions Tina didn't want to answer, not when she had to be "on" for the whole evening. She just had to get through tonight. That would be the worst part. Tomorrow she would review the campaign with Charmaine and plan for the next quarter. The following day she could go home.

She'd just slipped into her dress when the doorbell to her suite rang. *Madre mia.* Was it more flowers? Giorgio had sent two dozen yellow roses and Mamma, Angela and Francesca had all sent huge bouquets plus half a dozen bottles of Dom Perignon. Clearly they were coming ready to party.

The doorbell rang again, insistently. She hurried to open the door to Giorgio looking exceedingly handsome in a tuxedo while Layla and Angela were gorgeous in glittering evening gowns. Tina hugged and kissed them all and then went back around the circle for more hugs. "Oh, my God, I'm so glad to see you all!"

"Are you okay?" Giorgio asked, holding her away from him to study her face. "You look pale. Has the launch been too much for you? I knew we should have sent someone from the head office to oversee things."

"I'm fine," she assured him, dabbing her eyes. "The launch is going brilliantly. Everything is taken care of. The fashion show is going to be a huge success so you can just stop worrying and let your little sister have her moment of glory."

"I'm so excited about tonight," Angela said. "You saved us front row seats, I hope."

Tina smacked her forehead. "Will second row do? Sorry, there are so many others clamoring for the front row."

"She's teasing you," Layla said. "We'll stand in the back if you need more room for buyers or editors. We brought the painting. Giorgio, where is it?"

"Here, by the door." Giorgio picked up a large square package wrapped in heavy brown padded paper. "Do you want to have a look?"

A sharp pang pierced Tina's chest. She wanted this to be not just a parting gift, but a token to make up in some small way for the wrong she'd done Luke in not telling him the truth about who she was. It hurt to know she would never get to see her girl hanging next to Luke's boy. Would he even accept the painting from her or would he immediately give it away or sell it? She would likely never know. "I've seen it enough times. Don't unwrap it."

Smiling to ward off the tears, she ushered her family into the sitting area of her suite. "How about a champagne before I call the limo?"

She'd hoped to celebrate with both her family and Luke tonight, had planned to ask Luke to accompany her to the fashion show. That wasn't going to happen now. Their fling had started out so fun and spontaneous. How had things gone so wrong?

When flutes of Dom had been poured and toasts made, Tina turned to Giorgio seated next to her on the loveseat. "Fabio came to my boutique demanding money. I sent him away but I'm worried. Does he have any hope of this lawsuit being successful?"

"Not in the slightest," Giorgio said. "Our lawyers confirmed before we left Rome that he has no case against you. But if he's harassing you we should get in touch with the local police and take out a restraining order."

"That's what Luke said, but I don't think it's necessary. I'll only be here a couple more days. If he's still a problem when I'm in Rome then I'll act."

"Who's Luke?" Giorgio lowered his voice so Layla and Angela couldn't hear.

Tina was grateful for his discretion. "Just a man I got to know. He's the one I'm giving the painting to."

"Do you care for him?"

"I...yes, I do." She twisted the stem of her flute. "It was...intense for a while but now it's over." Those damn tears that had been so close to the surface all day started to seep through her lashes.

"*Cara*." Her brother took both her hands and squeezed tenderly. "You are too passionate. How do you lose your heart so easily? First Fabio and now this Luke."

"Luke is nothing like Fabio." Her feelings for him were so much deeper and stronger than anything she'd felt for the photographer. She couldn't believe now that she thought she'd ever loved him. "I resisted as long as I could, believe me. But Luke is a very special man." She sniffed and touched the corners of her eyes with a napkin and smiled. "Never mind. Let's not talk about him. Tonight is for celebration."

Thank goodness her family was around to lend her moral support. If she looked closely into her heart she knew she would see a small kernel of hope that Luke would, on reflection, forgive her and give her another chance. At the very least, she hoped he would see in her gifts a genuine love for him and a desire to make things right between them. After that, it was up to him.

Chapter Eleven

"I had to end it, right?" Luke slid another beer across the bar to Allan and cracked open his third since they'd started drinking only half an hour ago. There was a smallish group watching some tennis tournament, but Rosie was covering the bar. He wasn't normally a big drinker, but tonight he was going on a bender. All day he'd been trying to convince himself that breaking up with Tina was the only possible course of action under the circumstances. So far it hadn't worked because he kept thinking of all the good things about her. Now he was counting on Allan for reassurance. "She's a liar, not the kind of woman I'm looking for."

"Technically, she didn't lie. She simply omitted the truth. And aside from that, she's beautiful, sexy, smart, passionate and generous—if you'd bothered to cash her check," Allan mused as he searched the internet on his phone. "Hell, no, who would want someone like that?"

"Put that thing away and pay attention," Luke said.

"You're not being any help at all. And you're obviously not hearing me. She—"

"She's being sued for breach of promise by a creep called Fabio Donatelli," Allan said, reading off his phone. "I didn't even know you could still do that nowadays. His rap sheet includes charges over conning women in France, Italy and Spain. Handsome devil, judging by the photos, and apparently charming too, if the list of high society women who've been taken in by him are any indication. Most of them were too embarrassed to make an accusation. Until Tina. From what I gather, she shuns publicity of any personal nature." Allan glanced up. "You can add brave to her list of attributes."

"Let me see." Luke scanned the popular magazine article, getting angrier and angrier as he read all that Tina had been through. She'd told him only the barest details but not only had she been cheated and swindled by the man she'd thought loved her, then to add insult to injury, he'd sued her when she broke off their engagement. He, who'd committed criminal offenses. Luke wished he'd bashed his face in at the boutique when he had the chance. "His case will never stand up in court."

"That's not the point," Allan said. "He's harassing her. I'm not surprised she's wary."

"She told me her last boyfriend had used her, but I had no idea it was this bad," Luke said. "Why didn't she explain? I would have understood."

"How would she know that?" Allan sipped his beer. "Once bitten, twice shy. All this took place less than six months ago. And the lawsuit is recent."

"Oh, man." He'd accused her of trying to buy love. After

what she'd been through, that must have cut deep. Yes, he'd been angry and hurt, but he'd taken all his mommy issues and put them on Tina. In doing so he'd thrown away the best thing that had ever happened to him. "I'm an asshole."

"No, you're the most standup guy I know. Question is, what are you going to do to get her back? I presume you want her back."

"Hell, yeah. What can I do? She's at her fashion show tonight. It's really important to her. I don't want to barge in there and cause a scene." Luke pushed away his beer. Suddenly he had no interest in getting shit-faced.

"If I were you, I'd be trying like hell to get to her and tell her how much you appreciate her," Allan said.

"Appreciate? I'm going to tell her I love her. And she'd better not have a problem with that. Now, can I get a ticket to that damn fashion show or is it too late? They hold that at Bryant Park, right?"

"No, they moved it to Lincoln Center," Allan said, still reading off his phone. "I know someone who knows someone who works in management."

Luke clicked his fingers and a grin spread across his face. "Never mind. I just had a better idea."

• • •

Luke slipped his arms into the short black waiter's jacket and buttoned it up over the white shirt and black bow tie. The kitchen was bustling with chefs preparing canapés and waiters about to circulate with trays of food and drinks. The waiter he'd borrowed the jacket off had been only too happy to take a break. He just hoped he'd be able to find Tina among the hundreds of attendees at the cocktail party that would commence immediately following the fashion show.

A louder than usual burst of applause drew him to the door. His heart kicked up to triple time. Tina had come out onto the catwalk and was being presented with an enormous bouquet of flowers. Flashbulbs popped from the photographers. The models lined up on stage and paraded past her in a continuous line. Tina turned and gestured to them. The applause continued unabated.

In her red sequined dress, she was so beautiful it hurt his chest to look at her. If he was able to do nothing else, he absolutely had to apologize. He couldn't bear for their final conversation to be what went down at his apartment this morning, a bitter dialogue of accusations and recriminations. That wasn't what they were about.

Finally, Tina raised a hand. The crowd fell silent. "*Grazie, tutti, mille grazie*! Thank you all for coming tonight. And for your warm welcome to your beautiful city. Thank you to all the gorgeous models and to everyone involved in organizing the show, especially my New York agent, Charmaine Denton."

More applause. Again, Tina raised her hand. "I have a surprise tonight. During my stay in New York I've gotten to know a very special man who began a very special charity, the Disabled Children's Sports Foundation."

Luke straightened away from the door. What was she doing?

"Luke Pederson—" She broke off as a cheer went up. Smiling, she waited till the noise died away. "Luke not only gives generously of his money but also his time, coaching a boys' hockey team." Tina glanced at the closed, red velvet curtains behind her. "Luke's nephew Timmy is one of those boys. Timmy and his mother Stella have graciously agreed to appear tonight."

Through a break in the curtains, Timmy wheeled his chair, closely followed by Stella, who glanced awkwardly around then turned her focus back to her son. She was wearing an evening dress, no doubt one of Tina's designs, and inappropriately but endearingly, her adored scarf. Luke's eyes filled as Tina walked back to meet them and leaned down to kiss Timmy on the cheek. He barely heard what followed, his chest was so full and his ears were buzzing.

Stella began to speak, tentatively at first, then more confidently as the buzz of the crowd died down. "Tina, thank you so much for everything. I really appreciate it and I know the other parents will too. Our boys will be able to go to the playoffs they've been training so hard for. More kids will have opportunities in the future."

Luke opened his eyes to see Tina hugging his sister. Then she stepped back and applauded Stella and Timmy.

"Please, may I have everyone's attention." Tina raised her arms and the crowd quieted again. "The Borlenghi Boutique will donate thirty percent of all sales generated as a result of tonight's fashion show to the children's foundation. Timmy, you can tell your uncle that love can't be bought but good outcomes for kids like you, can. Thank you all, and have a very good night."

Eyes blurring, Luke clapped until his hands stung. Without a doubt Tina had the most generous heart he'd ever known.

"Hey, you," the head waiter called to Luke. "Grab a tray. In two seconds those people will be mingling, looking for refreshments."

· · ·

Tina clutched her empty cocktail glass, smiled and nodded as the Mayor of New York waxed lyrical about his policy of encouraging foreign investment in the city. The show had gone well and Stella and Timmy were a hit. Charmaine had initially panicked at essentially giving away the profits on an entire season of sales, but then she relented, as the buzz from the runway declaration created a wave of good press. The kind of press that would make the House of Borlenghi a household name in America. Tina was trending on Twitter with a veritable army of actresses vowing only to buy "clothes for worthy causes." *Dio*, perhaps she'd start a philanthropic trend. She had no desire for more publicity, but she'd do whatever was best for Luke's foundation. It would be days yet before the sales orders came in from the buyers and the chain stores but she was hopeful.

Giorgio, Layla, and Angela were out there in the crowd, enjoying the party. Every now and then she'd glimpse Angela's blond head or Layla's red curls, and wave. As for her, her smile was becoming increasingly forced. She was tired and her heart ached for Luke. She'd kept her eyes open for him, too, but he hadn't made an appearance. Their "fling" was over, she had to accept that.

"Champagne, madam? It's Dom Perignon, your favorite," a familiar husky voice said.

A prickle of awareness skittered over Tina's bare arms. She turned, her heart beating fast. Luke was wearing waiter's garb, his somber expression belied by the twinkle in his blue eyes. She plucked a flute of sparkling wine off the tray.

Her throat suddenly dry, she said, "You know your wines. Do you work here often?"

"Only the gala events." He lowered his voice. "You look beautiful tonight."

"Thank you." Was he role-playing or being genuine? He must be genuine. He could only have come here dressed like that for her. She glanced around. The mayor's ear had been claimed by a fashion blogger. It was just her and Luke, in a bubble of their own. Every cell in her body was telling her to throw herself into his arms, but he'd hurt her badly. Even though she'd hurt him, too, she'd learned to be cautious.

He came a little closer. "There's something I have to say before someone grabs you or the head waiter fires me for fraternizing with the guests."

"Go on." She sipped her champagne without tasting it. Everything, her entire future happiness, depended on this moment.

"Just to be very clear, I wish you were a salesgirl," he said in a low, urgent voice. "That's the woman I fell in love with. In fact, I wasn't happy to learn you had so much money. It's a hindrance to us being together, not a help. But as for this morning, I was wrong about you. You weren't trying to buy love. You're just a naturally generous person who wants to believe the best of people because you're so good and honest and true yourself. I'm sorry if I offended you. I-I have no right to expect it but I hope you can forgive me."

"Of course, I forgive you." She swallowed hard, feeling the ache in her chest. "I have trust issues," she said, searching his face. "I can't help it."

"Babe, I know what that's like." His voice vibrated with fervent emotion. "Maybe we can work through them together. One thing I want you to know, I will always be on your team. Always."

"Oh, Luke, I-I love you." Then a lump formed in her throat and she couldn't speak so she just nodded. Yes, to standing side by side, helping each other. Loving each other. Trusting.

"I read about that guy Fabio," Luke went on. "It's obvious you weren't to blame. He's a conman and if I ever get my hands on him he's going to regret the day he decided you were going to be his next victim."

"I'm so sorry I didn't trust you with the truth. I hope you can forgive me."

"It was understandable under the circumstances," he said gruffly. "I wish I'd dug deeper, earlier. I should have known you weren't the type to hide your identity without a good reason."

Tina managed a smile. "Oh, I don't know. Pretending to be a salesgirl hooked me up with a very hot carpenter." She smoothed a hand over his lapel and gave him a sultry gaze. "You look very sexy in that waiter's jacket. The champagne is nice but I would like your…full service."

"Pardon me," a fifty-something woman in a black cocktail dress interrupted in a pointed tone. "May *I* have a glass of champagne?"

"Certainly. Here you go." Luke handed the astonished woman the whole tray. Then he took Tina's hand and tugged her through the crowded ballroom. She waggled her fingers as she passed Angela. Her sister's eyebrows rose into her wispy bangs at seeing her leave with a waiter.

Tina laughed in delight as Luke led her through the tent and outside into the balmy evening. Then she stopped abruptly, dragging him to a halt. Lounging against a wall, smoking a cigarette, was Fabio. "*Merda!*"

"I'm guessing that's a swear word," Luke said grimly. "Just give me ten seconds with this guy." He started rolling up his sleeve.

"He's not worth it," Tina said. "Just walk past as if you don't even see him, as if he's nothing. Because that's what he is."

Fabio threw down his smoke and sauntered toward them. "So, Tina, you still have to pay for it," he smirked, then turned his gaze to look Luke up and down. "Only now you've taken to playing with the help."

If those insulting words weren't enough Fabio's smug look was all the excuse Luke needed to mess up that pretty face. He hauled his fist back and let fly with a right hook that had landed him time in the penalty box on more than one past occasion. His bunched knuckles smashed into cartilage and bone, sending the other man sprawling, his nose bloodied. Fabio spat blood onto the concrete and let loose an angry stream of Italian.

"Save it for the judge," Luke said, standing over him. "Don't you *ever* bother Tina again, or you'll have to go through not only me but the entire team of the New York Rangers. And those guys aren't half as gentle as I am." He turned to Tina and offered her his arm. "Shall we?"

Grinning, she hooked her arm through his. "You are one bad ass hockey player."

Luke pulled her to a halt next to the lit up fountain and pulled her into his arms to kiss her so thoroughly she had to cling to his neck to stay upright. The dancing waters, the starry night, the champagne…and the most wonderful man in the world. Could anything be more romantic?

She was floating as they crossed the plaza arm in arm and descended the steps to where Frank stood next to Tina's waiting limousine. Frank held the door open, not blinking an eye even though he must have seen the altercation with Fabio, not to mention the kiss. "Good evening, Tina. Sir."

"This is Luke." Tina climbed in after him and snuggled close. "My hotel?"

"My place." He traced her mouth with a fingertip. "Our place. *La mia casa è la tua casa.*" He gave Frank the address.

"*Molto bene*," she said, delighted. "You'll make an Italian yet."

"That's all part of my master plan."

"Then you'll come to our family holiday on the yacht in Naples?" She pressed tiny kisses to his jaw, his mouth, his nose. "Seaman First Class Pederson."

His arms went around her and pulled her close. "*Captain* Pederson has a nicer ring to it."

"You can practice your knots when you tie me up," she whispered in his ear. Then she tickled him till he caught her fingers and kissed them one by one, taking her baby finger into his mouth to slowly suck.

He claimed her lips next with a kiss that was firm and warm. His hand found her breast, caressing her in the darkness. "I'll go anywhere, do anything, to be with you."

Tina captured his hands and held them still. In the dim backseat she searched the shadows of his face. "Will you call your mother and wish her Happy Birthday?"

He hissed in a breath. "You drive a hard bargain."

"Please, Luke. You gave me another chance. Give her one too."

"You gave me a second chance when I didn't deserve it. I guess that's what love is all about." He brought her hands to his mouth and kissed them. "All right. I'll call her."

Tina put her arms around his neck and her words were muffled in his neck as she kissed him over and over. "You won't regret it."

As the limo pulled into the traffic and the privacy window rolled up with a whir, he turned to Tina. "Now where were we?"

Epilogue

Six weeks later...

Luke stood on the stepladder positioning Tina's painting of the girl in the forest so it faced the painting of the boy over the fireplace. She'd given it to him the day after the fashion show, but they'd been so busy they'd only now gotten around to hanging it.

"A little to the left. Not that far." Tina waved her hands as if conducting a symphony. "A touch to the right. Stop! *Perfetto*."

He marked the point on the wall then set the painting on the mantelpiece while he hammered in the picture hook. With the painting hung, he climbed down, put his arm around Tina's shoulders, and they stood back to view the result. The woods and the lighting were so cleverly done that they gave the illusion that the girl and the boy were just about to meet.

"They really do belong together, don't they?" Luke said.

"They look happy now," Tina agreed. "Before they looked a bit sad."

"I'm happy now too." He turned to her, searching her face. "Are you?"

"*Sì*, happier than I've ever been." She touched his face. "Do you really have to ask?"

Not really. Everything was going so well. The bar and the boutique were both doing a roaring business. The foundation had donations pouring in as a result of Tina's publicity the night of the fashion show, and his interviews on ESPN with the morning show Mikes. After that exhibition game with his old teammates, the owners were reaching out across the league, and it looked like the entire NHL might organize more exhibition games for charity regionally. His foundation wasn't just surviving—it was thriving!

He'd been to Italy and met Tina's family. Her mother and sisters were all wonderful, and he got along with Giorgio like a house on fire. Tina and Stella were in cahoots over a ready-to-wear line of practical but stylish everyday clothing that Tina would introduce into the major stores like Bloomingdales.

Best of all, he'd reconciled with his mother. Tina had gone with him to their first meeting at a coffee shop. Not surprisingly, his mom had taken a liking to his feisty Italian. Tina had coaxed out his mom's story and smoothed over the rough spots. Mom was in counseling and swore she hadn't gambled in eighteen months. Tina thought she was telling the truth and Luke was willing to believe. If she fell off the wagon, well, he would help her get back on.

Yes, life was pretty damn good. He and Tina spent most of their time together, either in Rome or New York, but inevitably there were many days apart too. He could live with that as long as they were solid. But despite their growing love they had yet to make permanent commitment. He wanted to change that.

"Tina." He swallowed, feeling a huge lump in his throat. He'd thought about this moment for days. He'd planned different scenarios, written scripts for himself, imagined the most romantic setting he could think of. This wasn't it but somehow the moment had come. He took a huge breath. "Will you marry me?"

Her startled gaze lifted to his. "Are you serious?"

He nodded.

"Luke, I love you so very much, but…" She was silent a moment. "Do you truly love me?"

He tucked a long curling strand of dark hair behind her ear. As if he hadn't said it a million times already. "You know I do."

"Would you love me if I was penniless?"

He smiled fondly as she segued into what had become a familiar ritual dialogue that invariably preceded their sexual role playing. "I would."

"Would you love me if I was a blonde with an overbite?"

"Absolutely. I'd be your dentist."

She glanced at him from beneath her thick lashes, coy and sexy. "Would you love me if I was say, a milkmaid and you were a farm boy?"

"I would. I would love you if you were a damsel in distress and I was a fireman." He brushed the curve of her breast but his heart sank a little. He'd proposed and she'd left him hanging. After all this time did she still see him primarily as a sex partner? "You know I'm always up for a little fun. What will it be then, milkmaid and farm boy?"

She gazed at him shyly. "How about bride and groom?"

Luke heard the tremor in her voice, that hint of her vulnerability she still hadn't completely overcome. His heart ached with love for her. He would make it his life's work to never let her feel less than worthy of the best he had to offer. His own voice trembled as he said, "I take it that's a yes."

"Sì. A thousand times over." She rested her head on his chest and for a long moment he held her close. At last she eased back, blinking. "We'll have to take a rain check on the farm yard frolic, though. We're meeting Stella and Timmy for roller skating."

"Right, I'd forgotten." Luke made no move to get ready. Instead he started unbuttoning Tina's blouse to see what kind of lacy bra she was wearing today.

Tina giggled. "What are you doing?"

"I'm celebrating our engagement. Mmm, pale green and pink." He lowered his mouth to the swell of breast above the lace and satin.

"Stella and Timmy…" Tina protested but unconvincingly as she slid her hands beneath his shirt and over his ribs.

"Milkmaids and damsels in distress are all very well," Luke murmured as he undid the snap on her jeans. "But I like it best when you play a bossy Italian sales assistant. Text Stella and tell her we'll be late."

Acknowledgments

I'd like to thank Vanessa Mitchell, my editor on this project, for her insight, ideas and hard work. She was invaluable in helping make TURNING THE TABLES the best it could be.

Grazie mille to Kati Tempesta, my Italian teacher, who helped me with the Italian words and phrases and made sure I used them correctly.

About the Author

Joan Kilby is the award-winning author of over twenty-five contemporary romance novels. Joan likes to immerses herself in her characters' world. For her current series *The Italian Connection* she's taking Italian lessons and growing vegetables used in Italian cuisine to indulge one of her hobbies—cooking. It will come as no surprise that her new favorite drink is pinot grigio. When she's not working on a book she can often be found at the gym doing yoga or at a local café indulging in her favorite pastime of people watching.

Discover **The Italian Connection** *series...*

MAKING OVER THE BILLIONAIRE

Designer Layla Langham is on a mission to convince the House of Borhlenghi to buy her designs. Now she's been given a chance at her dream... but only if she "lures" reclusive and work-obsessed (and really, *really* hot) billionaire Georgio Borlenghi to his family's yacht in Capri. With her career on the line and a very sexy Italian in her sights, each night with Georgio becomes a lesson in seduction and pleasure. But now the only way to achieve her dream is to lose the man she's falling for...

Also by Joan Kilby

MAD ABOUT YOU